Keeping

Promises

C. M. Lockhart

Written in Melanin Publishing
Established • 2019

Keeping Promises

Copyright © 2021 by C. M. Lockhart

For information contact:

http://www.WrittenInMelanin.com

Cover Design by Tajae Keith

Second Edition: November 2021

To Ma, Daddy, and E.

I wouldn't be who I am without y'all.

PART 1 – JASON

Loving Jason has always been the easiest and hardest thing I've ever done. Being in love with him came so naturally to me that I couldn't stop, even when I wanted to. The problem though, was that he was always just out of my reach.

He was never mine to love.

I knew that. From the very beginning, I knew it. And I knew that I could do nothing about it – nothing except for love him as completely as the way I did. Loving Jason was a rollercoaster ride I couldn't stop – a wave I couldn't surf – a pain I couldn't make not hurt. Knowing that didn't make it any easier to let him go. In fact, it just made it harder.

Jason made it so hard – nearly impossible – for me to let him go.

But I can't place the blame solely on him. I wanted to love Jason. I loved, loving Jason. He was a fourth slice of birthday cake – a full bag of Halloween candy – just a little too much of a bad decision to be considered a guilty pleasure. But I've been known to be unable to resist a bad idea – and Jason was by far the worst one – but he was the temptation that I gave into, every single time. And whenever I thought I had learned my lesson – when I felt that the pain was too big a burden to carry any longer – Jason would remind me of why I put up with so much of his shit to begin with.

Jason needed me.

He had an uncanny way of worming his way back into my good graces. It was never his whispered words of vulnerability in front of covered ears and averted eyes that pulled me back in. No, what kept me anchored to his side were those unspoken moments when he reached out for me, acting on an instinct he was never aware of.

Don't get me wrong, I enjoyed our secret rendezvouses – when he would hold me close, kiss me softly and whisper in my ear how much he needed me. But it was the moments when he ignored all the other people in his life who were so eager to comfort him in his time of need, and he reached out for me that let me know that loving him was something I couldn't stop doing.

In those moments, I felt I had something the rest of the world didn't. And I did.

I had Jason.

Chapter 1
So, I saw him again.

"Hey."

The voice was soft and closer to my ear than I ever thought it would be again. I felt his presence more than I heard his greeting, but still – I'd have known the sound of his voice anywhere. It was the voice of a man I had known in what now seemed like a different life. Back when my feelings for him were still new, and fresh, and just being with him was exciting.

Back then life hadn't happened to us yet, and that was the beauty of everything.

It's funny to me how all those memories from high school are already like faded photographs packed away in my mind, but every moment I spent with him was as crisp and clear as the day it happened. It wasn't hard to recall his lopsided grin on the first day of school – my dad teaching him how to shave in the hall bathroom – his crappy parking on the street in front of my house. That voice behind me belonged to the only man I had ever called my best friend so, of course I remembered him.

Jason wasn't the type of person to be forgotten.

I would never describe myself that way. In fact, I'd always felt if someone were to be forgotten, it would be me. Quiet and insecure have always been the adjectives that followed me – the kind of girl who disappeared if you weren't paying close attention. I'd always preferred it that way, but Jason saw me. He drifted into my lane like there were no lines on the road to guide him and I forgot there was any other way to be than with him.

We became inseparable.

I treasured every day that we walked home together from the bus stop and the hours we spent on the front porch talking until his mom picked him up. Even on the rainiest days, Jason was more than happy to spend it inside with me – playing video games, watching cartoons, and whispering about the deepest secrets of our lives. We told each other everything and we lived every moment we could together.

Life with Jason was good, but it was also unforgiving.

As time went on, he grew into a handsome,

popular athlete and I – well, I stayed in my lane. I was still the same quiet and insecure girl. That didn't change just because we got a little taller and advanced a few grades. But the easy relationship we'd always had was gone – instead becoming a tangled mess of complicated emotions we didn't know what to do with.

It was more than either of us could handle.

We were too young – too jealous and rash and hurt and angry. We loved each other too much in a place and a time that just wasn't right for us.

And trying to make it work, broke us.

I glanced behind me to confirm what I already knew and smiled. He was taller now and I was unable to keep my eyes from drifting over the muscle in his arms and the width of his shoulders before settling on his face. He still had the same lopsided grin I'd known my entire life with the same clear brown eyes staring down at me and the same full lips I'd loved to kiss. There was no mistaking him for anyone else.

He wasn't wearing anything fancy – just jeans with a gray shirt, but he didn't need to dress up. He was the type of man who could make a flour sack look like an Armani suit. He'd already caught the attention of two of the baristas behind the counter and I felt their eyes on us as he wrapped his six-two frame around me in a hug that left me feeling more warm and secure than a blanket in winter.

"Hi, Jason."

He paid for my drink after ordering his and we stepped outside to sit at one of the wrough iron tables. We were at the coffee shop a few blocks down from my apartment. It was a small place called *Coffee Cakes* and I indulged in a cup from them more often than I probably should. In the nearly two years I'd come to this place though, this was the first time I was meeting up with Jason.

I couldn't stop looking at him as we settled across from each other. I wanted to commit every new detail of his face to memory, but whenever I looked over at him, I saw him staring right back at me. We'd been together for less than a minute and already my heart was on a mission to beat every last breath out of my lungs. To say that keeping a calm face was a struggle would be an understatement.

I hated that Jason still made my heart race.

Getting flustered just from being near him made me want to shake some sense into myself.

I didn't want to feel anything for him. I shouldn't feel anything for him. I'd spent years trying to force myself to let him go and make space in my head and in my heart for someone new. But, to feel my heart running marathons that left me short of breath and a bit light headed – I knew without a doubt that I'd failed. I felt like I was robbing a younger version of myself of genuine feelings that should have started fading the day we parted ways. Wrong or not though, all the feelings I had for Jason that had been shoved down and locked away inside my heart were running rampant inside my chest.

It was a challenge to keep up my ladylike façade as I sat across from him when I truly wanted nothing more than to launch myself into his arms again.

"It's been a long time," he said. "I can't believe that I'm actually across from you right now." He shook his head, the disbelief written across his face. He seemed happy though and I smiled back at him, but I didn't say anything. I couldn't. It was taking everything in me to process the same thing that he was. Jason – my Jason – was sitting across the table from me.

Although, he wasn't mine anymore and he hadn't

been for a long time. But that didn't matter though. Because in this moment, it felt like he was. It felt like this was normal for us. Like this was how our lives were meant to turn out. Like I was meant to sit across from Jason on a sunny Saturday morning, with coffee in my hands and a smile on my face. This was the future I'd always wanted – this was the dream I wanted to be my reality.

"It's been a while," he said. He was repeating himself and I heard the little bits of laughter in his words. I knew he was just as nervous as I was. Somehow, knowing that made me relax. I wasn't the only one meeting my first love again. So, I nodded and laughed with him.

"It has."

"I didn't think you would actually agree to meet up with me. How have you been?"

"Good," I replied. "And you?"

"I've been good."

That was all it took for the floodgates of conversation to open. The atmosphere that had been thick with tension and nerves dissolved into a bubble of reminiscence and laughter. Jason told me stories of his undergraduate years at school in California and how he and Lucas had followed through on starting a business together. It had been a long-held dream of theirs and now Jason was a software engineer and Lucas was a computer programmer – they worked together to create applications and sold them to the companies that hired them.

I sat for a while just studying his face, taking in the changes and enjoying the sound of his voice. I hadn't realized how much I missed the sound of him talking until now. I'd done my best to convince myself that I stopped caring about Jason – that he was just a part of my past – but sitting in front of him reminded me just how much of a liar I was.

I had missed him every day he'd been gone.

Even now, I could tell that while he was still the same Jason I fell in love with, he was different. His face was a little wider – his teeth weren't as white – he was cleanshaven now. The muscles in his arms weren't as thick as when he was on the football team. But his smile was just as infectious as it had always been, and the way his eyes never left my face as he talked made me feel like there was nothing in the world he wanted more than to be here with me.

"So, Kay," he said, leaning back in his chair,

"what have you been up to in the last five years?"

That's right – it has been five years since things ended between us.

"I've been living," I joked. We shared a smile as I met his eyes again. It was my turn to talk, so I told him about how I chose to go to an HBCU and majored in business management and marketing – that I came here once with my friend to visit and fell in love with the place – that I started freelancing as a social media consultant just before graduation and moved to Atlanta after I'd built up a portfolio of a few steady clients. I told him all the little tidbits of my life that he missed out on, and his eyes never left mine. Not even for a second.

His gaze had always been intense, and I felt my face grow hot as he studied me. I looked away from him as I sipped from my nearly empty cup. After putting it back on the table, I met his eyes again.

"So, yeah," I took a deep breath and shrugged, "that's my life. And no one calls me 'Kay' anymore."

"Really?" He raised an eyebrow. "That's surprising. Everyone used to call you that."

"It's by design," I replied.

The words were simple, but they carried the

weight I had intended them to. Despite how light I felt at seeing Jason – how clear it became that I still loved him – we had a history that had weighted my heart down with bricks for years and I wasn't going to pass up the opportunity to chuck a few of them at him. I wanted him to know that behind the warmth of the smile in front of him, was an anger that – despite my best efforts – still sparked to life at the sight of him.

He sighed and rubbed at his chin. That was a new habit.

"You still mad at me?"

I looked away from him. "I wouldn't say that. I was actually never mad at you. Hurt would be the better word." I shrugged and sat back in the chair. "But we can't undo what happened. I could only try to move on from it. So, I did."

"Without me."

"I had to give up on one of us," I said.

I looked away from him thinking about the night I'd walked away from him. I had cried all night – to the point where my chest was so tight, I couldn't draw a full breath. My eyes were swollen – my pillows were soaked through – I'd exhausted myself beyond anything I could have imagined – and I had no one to turn to. I was truly alone for the first time in my life and all I could imagine in my future was an endless stretch of emptiness. That night, just existing in my own space had felt too painful a task to endure.

I never had the pleasure of forgetting what Jason put me through.

"I shouldn't have taken Alice to prom."

My heart skipped at the name. Alice Mayben. She was the proverbial straw that broke the camel's back. Jason and I had too many problems to count – I'd never pretend we didn't – but Alice Mayben had been the worst of them. I sighed and rolled my eyes. This was not a part of our past I wanted to dredge up.

"You made your choice."

"It was the wrong one."

"It's the one you have to live with."

"It's one of my biggest regrets," he said. He leaned forward, locking his eyes onto mine. "I've said it a million times but hear me this time. I'm sorry, Kay." He sighed, "I was so caught up in being the guy everyone wanted me to be, I didn't realize I'd lost the person who mattered to me the most until it was too late."

I looked at him – really looked at him as I processed his words. Even with the years between us, I knew that his apology was sincere. After hearing it though, I also knew that the apology – while appreciated – wasn't what I wanted. It was never that I hadn't heard his pleas and apologies before, it was just that, alone, they were never enough to fix what he'd broken. I'd done my best to forgive Jason and move forward with my life, but the pain and anger he left me with was a tether to the past I could never break free of. I'd tried filling my days with the love of someone else, praying it would be enough to release me of everything that held me back. It wasn't until I was alone again – too exhausted to even put up a fight anymore – that I finally understood.

I couldn't run from it.

Not from what I felt.

And seeing Jason only served as a reminder of all the love I still had for him. All the anger I'd carried with me was nothing more than cooled embers now – I'd long since given up on feeding it.

"Thank you for the apology," I said with a small smile, "but like I said, we can't undo the past. I put that whole matter behind me a while ago."

"But you never called me back."

I shook my head. "No. And if we hadn't met up here today, I still wouldn't have."

"I'm glad I showed up then."

I nodded and giggled. "You know what? I'm glad you did too."

Silence fell over our table, and I stood from my seat. Seeing Jason had given me some closure – enough to finally, maybe, let him go – and it was clear that our visit had run its course. I picked up my empty cup and smiled at him.

"I'm glad you're doing good, Jason. I'll see you later."

"Three weeks."

I paused and let my eyebrows pull together. "What?"

"I'll have another free weekend in three weeks. Can I see you again and buy you another coffee? Breakfast maybe?"

"That's not a good idea," I said.

"And since when has that ever deterred Kamry Marshall?"

I bit back a laugh and thought it over. I didn't see any real harm in getting a free breakfast – it was far less dangerous than dinner – so, ignoring my better judgement that was advising me against it, I nodded my head.

"Fine. Three weeks it is."

CHAPTER 2
NOW, I'M TELLING THE WHOLE LESS THAN SOBER TRUTH.

"Jason was rain on a sunny day," I said. "Snow in the spring. A warm breeze on a front porch with laughter caught in the back of your throat as you watch the cars go by."

"What the hell does that mean?"

"It means," I giggled, "that he was mysterious and unexpected and," I paused and sighed, "a feeling that I never wanted to let go of."

"I have no idea what the hell you're talking about or who Jason is."

Lana sighed and laid her head back on the couch. She was mostly drunk and a little high – so was I. We were in her apartment having a night in together. It was something we did on a regular basis, but this was the first time in a long while I had too many words flooding my mind to keep my mouth shut. Under normal circumstances, we'd order food and sit by the pool downstairs until it arrived before stuffing our faces and ultimately falling asleep on her couch, but tonight was different.

I needed to talk.

I walked over to the couch and passed her a refilled drink of vodka and lemonade before flopping down next to her. We sipped in silence before I looked at her.

"I guess I never told you about him."

"We've all got our secrets," she said.

"I guess," I said. "I saw him this afternoon."

"Jason?"

I nodded. "Yeah. And he looks really good."

With no warning, tears started rolling down my cheeks. Lana jumped up and tried to ask if I was okay, but I just laughed. I laughed and laughed until a sob broke through and I tried to smile at her.

"I've avoided him for five years, and I'm still in love with him," I whispered through a cracked voice. "I still love him, and it hurts so damn much!"

I lost all the composure I had, and I cried over Jason in a way I hadn't let myself since the night he shattered my heart. I gasped for air and swiped at the tears, but there was no stopping them. It had been years in the making and I couldn't push away all the emotions that came with knowing Jason that I had ignored.

Lana watched me in shock, and I couldn't blame her. I was bawling on her couch, dissolving into a puddle of tears over a man she'd never even heard of five minutes ago. We'd been friends since our freshman year of college, but she'd never seen me so weak before – so broken that I couldn't even bring myself tell her what was going on. The person she knew was strong and detached – a woman who didn't get tangled in strings or within throwing range of a romantic risk. The woman she knew put insurmountable amounts of emotional distance between herself and every man who approached her. She didn't know that I had once been the girl who loved harder than anyone else – that I'd lost my heart long before I met her – that the woman she knew was only a single intact piece of the girl I had been.

She didn't know about Jason and she didn't know that he was the only one who could break me.

She put her arm around me and tried to console me, but this was something like a virus – a thing that needed to run its course. It took a while, but I calmed down. After catching my breath, she gave me some water – then some lemonade and vodka – then a little more to smoke. Then we sat on her couch – a little too not sober to care that we weren't.

"I'm sorry, Lana."

The words were soft, but she heard me anyway and shook her head.

"Don't apologize. I wish I had known that you were hurting like this though."

"It's not a thing you really greet people with, you know? Like, 'hi, I'm Kamry and I'm emotionally stunted because the only boy I've ever loved broke my heart and I can't get over it. Nice to meet you. Hope we can be great friends.'" I said it as a joke and we laughed, but I seriously hadn't had any idea how to tell people who didn't know Jason, about Jason. Where would I have even started? Our story went back so far – it would take hours to tell it all and I wasn't exactly eager to relive it.

"I never told you," I said, "because I didn't want to remember." I sighed. "I lied when I said that I never had a boyfriend before."

Lana looked like she was remembering the conversation. She'd asked me back in college when our friendship was still new, and she couldn't understand why I turned down any guy that tried to get serious with me. I hadn't been unsociable – I just didn't let any strings become attached, and she thought the reason was because I had a boyfriend waiting for me back home. I'd shrugged off her question and told her that there was no one waiting for me and that I'd never had a boyfriend. She always let me know that she didn't believe me – that a girl who was as pretty and socially acceptable as I was couldn't have been single her entire life. She never pushed for the truth though. She knew it was a lie, and she let me tell it.

Jason was my lie.

But now, it's time for the truth. I settled into the couch and she waited patiently as I prepared myself to tell the story of the boy I loved into a man and left behind.

"Jason wasn't my boyfriend," I told her, "but we loved each other more than most people ever do."

Chapter 3
I met him in the second grade.

"Hi. I'm Jason."

These were the first words I ever heard from Jason Orion Lipsky. We were starting the second grade and it was my first day going to Kimner Elementary School – my first day riding the school bus – and what I remember as the first day of the rest of my life. My mom stood on the front porch – watching to make sure that I got to the bus stop okay by myself. Jason was waiting there with a giant grin on his face for a reason I would never know. He had on jean shorts and a plain blue shirt and his hands were gripped around the straps of the bookbag on his back. As I walked up, he held out his right hand to me. I was a bit startled, but I shook his hand anyway.

"Hi. I'm Kamry."

"Nice to meet you! What grade are you in?"

And just like that, Jason was suddenly in my

life. Before the bus had even arrived, I knew that he lived four houses down from mine on the opposite corner of the street – he had waffles that morning for breakfast and his mom dropped him off at the bus stop on her way to work – his favorite color was purple and he didn't care if everyone told him it was a color for girls. From the moment we stepped onto that bus, it seemed like we were always sat next to each other. Mrs. Gail assigned us the same seat on the bus – Mr. Allen put us at the same table in the cafeteria to wait for our class to be called – Miss Amber put us in the same group. Our class was arranged in alphabetical order and Jason sat across from me.

Michelle McFarlan sat to my left and Lucas Pars sat in front of her.

At the time I had no way of knowing that this seating arrangement would allow me to have three of the best friends I would ever hope to have – and that it would lead me to loving the boy sitting across from me more than I loved myself. There was no way to know that – we were just kids in the second grade. Jason was my first friend and all I knew was that I was grateful to him that I wouldn't have to go through school alone.

The rest of the day felt magical to me.

Michelle and I clicked right away, and by the time recess came around after lunch, we were as thick as thieves. So, when Jason called out that I was "it" during a game of tag, Michelle was right with me tracking people down. It was clear that Michelle was faster than most of the kids in the class, because she had no problems chasing down half of them on her own.

Jason was too fast for her though – always a half step out of reach.

It wasn't long before Michelle was out of breath and standing with her hands on her knees – frustration written all over her face. Jason grinned and taunted her, but there was nothing she could do about it. She couldn't catch him – but she wasn't the only one who was trying to.

Michelle's eyes were bright with vengeance as she pointed to him.

"Get him, Kamry!"

That was all she said, and I took off after him. His eyes widened before he sprinted away. Michelle was fast, but I was even faster and the gap between us closed in seconds. Jason did his best to avoid me

– running through the swings – under the slides – to the other end of the playground where the fence separated us from the fifth graders. He ran along it for as long as he could, but like fences tend to do – it met at a corner and before he could make the sharp turn to the left, I cornered him with a laugh.

"I caught you, Jason."

His eyes glanced around, and he tried to make a quick escape, but I threw my arms around him and we both fell to the ground in a fit of laughter.

"Okay. You caught me," he admitted. He stood from the ground and offered me a hand up before we walked back to where our class was lining up.

"That was fun."

"Yeah," I agreed. "You're 'it' next time."

"Only if you want to lose," he joked.

I scoffed. "There's no way you're going to catch me."

"I will," he said with confidence.

I rolled my eyes at him before running to catch up with Michelle, who was waiting for me at the back of the line. The rest of the day passed in a blur and soon we were on the bus headed back home. Lucas was a car rider, but Michelle rode the same bus we did in the afternoons, so she sat in the seat in front of us.

We didn't stop talking until she got off. There were three bus stops between her stop and ours. Jason and I were one of the first ones to be picked up in the morning, so we were also one of the last to be dropped off. We waved to Mrs. Gail before walking down the steps. My mom was waiting on the front porch for me – as she'd promised she would be that morning – and waved to me as the bus pulled off.

"I have to go now," I said to Jason, "but I'll see you tomorrow."

"Yeah. Okay." His words were half-hearted, and his eyes were searching the street. I looked around too before turning back to him.

"What are you looking for?"

"My mom. But," he said, his voice dropping, "I don't see her."

"Oh." I bit my lip as I looked at him. I had to walk home – my mom was starting to look impatient and I didn't want to get in trouble. But I didn't want to leave Jason alone at the bus stop either.

"I'll be right back," I told Jason.

I jogged down the street and up the front steps to my house where my mom was waiting. She smiled and hugged me while asking how my first day went. I hugged her back and gave her the highlights of my day before pointing to the bus stop.

"That's Jason," I told her, "and his mom isn't here to pick him up yet. Can he wait here with us until she comes?"

"He can't just come to our house Kammie," she said. "His mom will worry about him if he's not where she told him to be when she comes to get him."

"Oh."

She smiled and slid my bookbag from my shoulders. "Let's take your things inside first, and then we can go wait with him. How's that?"

"Okay!"

Less than five minutes later, we were all waiting at the bus stop for Jason's mom. My mom brought him one of the little bottles of water we had, and Jason shook my mom's hand. He introduced himself to her just like he had to me that morning, and she shook his hand with a smile.

We ended up waiting for over an hour before Jason's mom finally arrived. She pulled her little red car to the side of the road and rushed out with an apologetic look on her face. Jason ran up to her, threw his arms around her waist and hugged her as tight as he could. She hugged him back before looking at my mom.

"Hi. I'm Karolyn Marshall," my mom said extending her hand. "I take it you're Jason's mother?"

"I am," she said, shaking my mom's outstretched hand. "Amana Lipsky."

"Nice to meet you. This is my daughter, Kamry," she said putting her hand on my shoulder. "Her and Jason are in the same class apparently, and she asked if we could wait with him until you got here."

"I see," she said. She turned a big grin towards me. "Thank you for being so kind to Jason."

I nodded and smiled. My mom asked if she could talk with her for a minute and Jason's mom agreed. She told Jason to get in the car and he waved at me before climbing into the backseat. My mom sent me on the walk back home, so I waved back at Jason before starting down the street. I waited on the steps for my mom to come back. I couldn't tell what they were saying, but our moms continued talking for what felt like a long time before they went their separate ways.

Jason's car rode down the street in the opposite

direction and pulled into a driveway that wasn't far from our house. My mom stopped at the bottom of the steps and laughed at me for waiting on her.

"What are you doing out here? You should be inside with your dad already."

"I know."

I wanted to ask her what the conversation was about. The words were burning on the tip of my tongue, but I knew better than to ask – that was "grown folks' business" as my mother would say. If I had been meant to be part of the conversation, she wouldn't have sent me away. But still – I wanted to know.

I guess I couldn't hide my curiosity, because she smiled and placed her hand on top of my head. "Jason will be walking home with you, starting tomorrow. He's going to wait here with us until his mom comes to get him. Is that okay?"

My face lit up and I nodded. "Yes!"

She laughed. "I thought you'd be okay with it. Make sure you help me clean up tonight before he comes over."

"Okay."

That decision was only the first of many that

would set Jason up to become – what I thought would be – a permanent fixture in my life.

CHAPTER 4
HE WAS MY BEST FRIEND & I LOVED HIM.

After that first day in the second grade, Jason became so much a part of my life, that I no longer knew what it meant to be without him. We rode the bus together in the mornings – we sat together in class – we ate lunch at the same table and played together at recess. We walked home together and then repeated it all the next day. And every day with him was wonderful because Jason was funny and kind and always grinning – and I was six going on seven and you don't get tired of being around someone like that.

At least, I didn't.

I never got tired of Jason. In fact – had my parents allowed it – I would have never let Jason leave. I always wanted to be with him, and it was great because he always wanted to be with me too. At that point in my life, I had never known what it felt like to be picked – to be wanted – to be the designated other half of a pair and I couldn't get enough of that feeling.

I was six going on seven until the day I turned seven going on eight.

Jason came to my birthday party with Michelle and Lucas and a few of my cousins. It wasn't anything fancy – just a backyard party with games and music, cake and ice cream. It was one of the best birthday parties I can remember having, and Jason was the first one there and the last one to leave. The party was over once the sun started to go down – everyone else had gone home already, and his mom was sitting in the kitchen talking to my parents while they ate leftover cake and watched us from the window.

We were too tired to run around anymore, so we just sat on the sun-warmed steps of the deck and pretended like the fall breeze was just as warm as the summer one had been, because we weren't ready to go inside – not yet. We split the last slice of cake we were allowed to have – me eating the cake and him the icing – because I never liked store-bought icing – and for some reason, he loved it.

We had just finished it off when he looked at me. He stared at my face for a moment too long before blurting out his next words.

"Kay, you're my best friend."

I stared back at him for two reasons. One, because no one had ever called me Kay before. My parents called me Kammie, but Kay was a new one on me – and it sounded like something that would stick around. I'd started calling him Jay because that's what his mom called him, and something inside me lit up at the thought that the name he'd given me matched his own – it felt like we were partners in crime, and it sent tingles through my stomach when he said it.

The second reason I stared at him was because, we were seven. He was a boy and I was a girl, and he was telling me that I was his best friend. I wasn't all that surprised by his words – we were always together, and I did like him more than anyone else – but it felt like we were breaking some kind of unspoken rule. I kind of liked that too though – so I smiled back at him.

"Yeah. You're mine too."

"Cool."

That was the moment that set both of our lives on an irreversible collision with each other.

If time travelling were a thing, and I wanted to

stop myself from falling in love with Jason – this would be the moment I would try to prevent. Because, once we said we were best friends, that put him just a step above everyone else in my mind. It was a critical step though – had he missed it – my life would not have been what it was. Not loving him was no longer an option for me. Falling in love with him was already put into motion, and it wouldn't require any effort from him – it was only a matter of time.

But even if I could travel back to this moment, I still wouldn't stop it from happening. Even knowing what I do now – that this is the starting gun of a race where the winner will be me, and all I will get for my effort is a broken heart and a bucket of my own blood, sweat and tears that I put into loving him – I would still make the choice to be with Jason, because being Jason's best friend is something that I would never want to erase from my life.

We dissolved into a fit of giggles after that – and too soon it was time to go – but my story with Jason was still at the very beginning.

I thought I spent a lot of time with him before, but it was no match for how much I saw of him from then on. I started to forget what my days were like without him. Even when we weren't at school, we rode our bikes on the weekends or played video games inside. As we got older, we went to the neighborhood park, or he came with us out to eat, or we watched cartoons together – some days we didn't do anything but sit on the front steps and talk. It didn't matter what we were doing as long as we were doing it together.

I don't know why being together made so much sense to us – it just did.

It was like learning how to walk – clumsy at first, but then it was the only thing we knew how to do. And whenever I really thought about it, it made my heart beat fast because I knew that karma was real – that life wasn't fair – that where there are winners, there are losers, and I kept winning. I kept waiting for the inevitable curve ball that life would throw at me. Michelle would tell me to stop worrying and to just be grateful for my blessings – and I was – but I also knew that the scales were tipped too far in my favor.

And that terrified me because, I knew that Jason was not replaceable.

I learned that lesson when the roots of our friendship weren't very deep yet. Miranda had tried to start trouble between us. She spread rumors around our class that I was telling lies about Jason, and when I chose to sit with Michelle, Lacey, and Lindsey at lunch, she tried to convince him that I didn't want to be his friend anymore. I never paid attention to Miranda, but when Jason came over that afternoon, he wasn't his usual self. When I asked him about it, he locked his eyes onto mine and I was surprised by how serious he looked.

"We're good, right?"

"What are you talking about?"

"Well," he said, before repeating what Miranda told him. I listened to him and was stunned and a little angry that he believed her.

"Miranda is a liar. We're best friends."

"I thought so."

"You're stuck with me forever. If I change my mind, I'll tell you."

He held out his pinky finger, his normal grin back on his face. "Forever?"

"Forever," I said, wrapping my pinky around his.

"Sealed with a kiss," he whispered, pushing his thumb into mine. I laughed and pushed back – our kissing thumbs evolved into a thumb war and

Miranda's words became a forgotten problem that we were already over. But this would become a moment that neither of us would forget.

We only made three promises to each other that were sealed with a kiss, and that was the first one.

A promise between us was one thing, but a pinky promise sealed with a kiss was a different beast altogether – it was an unbreakable vow. In our world, there wasn't a promise that was more important than the one we made to each other that day, and for the next five years, it was the easiest promise to keep. Even as we grew older and second grade turned to third, then fourth, then fifth, everything was always the same with us. It wasn't until we got to middle school that things between us began to change.

It was around that time I realized that being away from Jason wasn't as terrible as I used to think it was. So, in the sixth grade, I stopped riding the bus in the mornings. Our middle school was closer to my dad's job, so he offered to drop me off in the mornings on his way to work and I took him up on it. This was the first bit of distance that was put between me and Jason – and I didn't hate it. In fact, I looked forward to the times I had my dad to myself and it was just us in the car with his music – it was that space in the car that I felt like I could talk to him about anything.

I needed that safe space with him, because Jason and I had gotten closer. I don't know how it happened, but it seemed Jason had become comfortable with casually touching me – his hand brushing mine on the table – his legs stretched out beneath his desk, nudging mine in class – an arm around my shoulders when we're walking. It didn't take me off guard at first – we used to wrestle and fight all the time, so him touching me wasn't unheard of.

I just became aware of how much he was doing it.

And I liked it.

My heart raced whenever our skin came into contact. I was eleven going on twelve, and after a summer apart spent with me at camp and him at the beach, I was aware of the situation I was in. Distance makes the heart grow fonder and my heart was so fond of Jason that summer – it hurt. I didn't realize I could miss a single person as much as I did, even when I was busy and having fun – or maybe it was because I was busy and having fun. I wanted to share everything with him, and the other girls in my room had no trouble teasing me about how much we called each other.

I had the biggest crush on Jason Lipsky.

So, when I walked into Mr. Scales class that first day of seventh grade, my heart couldn't have been pounding harder. I already knew that we were in the same class, but I didn't know anything else – if he was at school yet – if he was in class already – if he'd saved me a seat or if it was assigned. So much was running through my mind that I almost didn't see Michelle when she threw her arms around me.

It was only then that I remembered that Jason hadn't been the only person I missed that summer.

I hugged her back, and in the blink of an eye, I was distracted from my worries of Jason and caught up in a conversation with Michelle about what happened while I was gone. Michelle's dad was from Georgia, so she always spent the summers with him there. We had just made it to Mr. Scales classroom and picked a few seats in the last row on the left side of the room when I saw Jason walk in. Michelle kept talking, but my heart stopped, and so did the conversation because Michelle turned to see why all my attention had left her.

She called to him and Lucas, but I didn't hear a word she said — I was already launching myself into his waiting arms with a giant grin on my face. I couldn't hide how excited I was to see him. I was happy to see everyone else too, but there was no comparing how much I wanted to see them to how much I had missed Jason. He wrapped his arms around me and squeezed back before lifting me off the floor.

I laughed, feeling lighter and happier than I had in the six-weeks we'd been apart.

"Hey, Kay."

My eyes widened and I took a step back to look at him. "When did your voice drop?"

He laughed and looked away from me with a shrug. "I don't know."

He was much taller than before and he was leaner, with a lot more muscle than I remembered him having. He had braces now and his voice had lowered — the sound of it made me shiver in a way that I didn't hate — and he smelled spicy and sweet, and my mind was already concocting ways to get his jacket from him before we even made it back to our seats.

"So, how was your summer?"

Jason asked the question, and it was aimed at the group, but Michelle and Lucas both turned their eyes to me like they knew something I didn't. Feeling like my answer was the one they were waiting for, I told them about my summer at camp. It was the first one I had ever been to, and I had what I felt to be an endless supply of stories to tell them. Before I could tell them everything, the bell was ringing, and it was time for us to take our seats for homeroom.

Not long after that, we were dismissed to our first class, and just like always, I found Michelle, Lucas and Jason waiting for me at the door. I caught up to them and as easy as breathing almost, Jason dropped his arm around me, and I slid mine around his back – and in that moment – I knew without a doubt that there was no turning back.

That crush I had on Jason – the one that everyone told me was just a crush because we were always together – because I would grow out of it – because I was too young to feel anything more than that – wasn't just a crush.

I wasn't weighted down – I was free falling.

CHAPTER 5
& THE BEAUTY WAS HE LOVED ME BACK.

On the thirteenth day of September, in our eighth-grade year, Jason Lipsky told me for the first time that he loved me.

And I believed him.

The day started out no different than any other. It was an early Saturday morning – Jason was at our house because his mom was working and together is where we wanted to be anyways. We were playing video games in my room and Jason was beating me in every round. I was frustrated because he made it look so effortless – and even though I liked how cool he was – I also hated how cool he was.

"How are you beating me?"

"I'm just better," he said with a smirk.

"Nah, I just suck at this game," I lied. The real problem was that I couldn't focus on the game.

"Sure," he said, setting his controller aside, "we'll

go with that."

"What are you doing?"

"I'm done playing."

"Not until I win!"

He shook his head and stood from the ground. "That's not going to happen. Let's go outside."

I thought about arguing with him, but the fire just wasn't in me. I didn't really care about the game — I just wanted to keep sitting close enough to him for our knees to touch. My lack of focus on the game was the only reason I kept losing, but I accepted the hand he offered me anyway, and let him pull me to my feet.

We walked down the hall to the front door, and I told my dad that we were going to the park as we passed him in his chair. He told us to be safe and we were on our way. Before we turned the corner that led to the park, Jason grabbed my hand and kept walking down the street.

"I left my basketball at home. Let's go get it real quick."

I looked at him with surprise but didn't argue with him. I didn't go to Jason's house often and when I did, I didn't go inside. My parents had a rule that I was only allowed inside when his mom was home, but she was a flight attendant so that wasn't very often. I'd only been through the front door maybe a half-dozen times in the six years we'd known each other, so just following him inside made my heart race – I wasn't the type of kid who disobeyed her parents.

"Um, Jay? I'll just wait outside."

Jason grabbed my hand again. "Just hang on a second. It's in my room. I'll grab it and we can go."

He hadn't flicked on the lights yet, and his skin on mine in the dark made my heart jump to my throat, and I yanked my hand back from his.

"Are you okay?"

"Fine," I nodded. "Just get your ball so we can go."

He turned and jogged up the stairs flipping light switches as he went. I waited with my back against the door, my heart pounding in my chest and my mind racing. I was nervous to be alone – truly alone – with Jason. I was breaking my parents' rule simply by being there, and my mind kept creating outlandish scenarios that kept me from calming down. I took deep breaths and tried to keep my cool, but Jason was back faster than I expected him to be.

"I'm ready."

"Great," I choked out, "then let's go."

"Seriously, Kay," he said, "are you okay? You look nervous."

"I am," I blurted out.

"Why?"

"Because we're alone in your house? I'm not supposed to be here."

"Does being alone with me bother you?"

"Of course not," I lied, "I just –"

"Kamry." Jason using my given name wasn't something that happened often, so I froze and met his eyes in the dim light of the hallway, and I realized that we were far closer than I thought. My lungs were struggling to function and all I could hear in my ears was my own heartbeat racing. I tried to take a step back, but I was already against the door, so I just waited. Jason took my hand again, slower this time.

"Do I make you nervous?"

"Why would you make me nervous?"

Even I could hear through my pitiful attempt to sound calm and I died a little bit from embarrassment. He grinned before laughing and in that moment, I heard it – he was nervous too. That laugh wasn't his normal laugh. His palm was sweaty.

He didn't have his basketball.

"Where's your ball?"

He looked down at his empty arm and then back at me with a blank look. "I forgot it."

We looked at each other before dissolving into nervous laughter. He was still holding my hand. My heart was still racing. I was confused. My brain couldn't keep up with what was happening.

"I have to tell you something Kay, but I don't want you to hate me."

"I could never hate you," I told him.

"I love you. Go out with me?"

I stared at him – shock written across my face. I couldn't fathom that this moment was real. Jason Lipsky was telling me that he loved me. Jason Lipsky was holding my hand and asking me out. Even in the best of my dreams I couldn't have imagined that. I dug the nails of my free hand into the center of my palm to confirm that I was awake – this moment was real and happening and Jason was in front of me saying those words.

I nodded. "Yes."

He blew out a sigh of relief and then without warning, he leaned forward and kissed me. He gave me his first kiss. He gave me my first kiss. We had our first kiss. I had no idea what to do.

And then it was over. It was too quick. Our eyes met and I squeezed his hand with a single whispered word.

"Again."

He grinned and pressed his lips to mine once more and this time, I kissed him back.

And all the years of being with each other seemed to explode in a single moment, because kissing Jason was better than every one of my favorite memories smashed together. Every second was better than the last and I couldn't get enough of it.

Kissing Jason was heaven.

We never ended up getting his ball or actually making it to the park. We just stood in his hallway – holding hands, kissing and living in a moment we thought would never come. It was awkward at first, but it was something that didn't take long for us to get used to. After a while, we walked back down the street to my house and sat on the front porch after I let my dad know we were back.

"So," I said as I took a seat next to him, "you're my boyfriend now?"

"Pretty sure, yeah."

I looked away and giggled. "Cool."

"You seem happy," he said.

"I could say the same about you."

He shrugged, but the grin on his face told everything. "Let's keep it to ourselves though."

"Why?"

"I don't know. I just don't want people asking us about it."

"Can I tell Michelle?"

"Michelle and Lucas don't count as people."

We both laughed and I agreed. It would be annoying to have people watching us and asking us about it – because that's what kids did in the eighth grade. Besides, it wasn't like much would be different between us anyway. The sun was setting, and I knew that Jason would have to go back home soon so I wrapped my pinky around his.

"You said you loved me?"

"Yeah."

I smiled, "I love you too."

"Forever?"

"Forever."

He glanced around before pressing his lips to

mine with a smirk. "Sealed with a kiss."

That was our second promise.

I spent the rest of the night on the phone with Michelle telling her everything that happened in excited whispers. She had a million questions, and I had a million answers for her, and it was probably the best night of my life. I was in love with Jason, and he loved me back, and he was my boyfriend, and I felt so light I could've floated straight into the stars if the roof hadn't kept me in.

CHAPTER 6
BUT, THINGS WERE NEVER THAT SIMPLE,

Life required balance and the scales were tipped too far in my favor.

I knew it – and I ignored it. I didn't want to think that the happiness I felt would ever come to an end. I didn't want to imagine what a life without Jason would look like – because I knew that a life without Jason was the only thing that could even out the scales for me. I was hopeful in thinking that Jason loving me wasn't a cruel joke that life would play on me. I was convinced that our story would not turn out to be a tragedy.

It didn't start out that way, but as things tend to do – they changed. We were still just kids, but we thought we knew what it meant to be in love.

We didn't.

I loved Jason so much, and what I felt for him was so raw and pure – I could never love anyone the way I loved him. He was my first love and as they say – that first love is the sweetest. Everything I felt for him was ripped from the depths of my soul and given to him alongside my every thought, my every smile, my every heartbeat – without hesitation. The single thought of him dominated my being because I was thirteen going on fourteen and I didn't know what it meant to have boundaries – to have parts of myself that were only for myself.

From the day that my lips first felt the softness of his, my heart was lost to anyone but him.

He held everything I was in the palm of his hand and I did not care. I was naive in thinking that he would never hurt me – could never hurt me – and that I would never hurt him – that there was no possible way for something as pure as what we had to be tainted.

The problem was, we fell into an in-between space where we weren't really together – but we weren't really not together either. We were more than best friends, but still somehow less than a couple. Somewhere along the line we became complacent – just knowing that we loved each other was enough for us. It was never anything that we had to shout to the world or have everyone know.

I don't know when that changed for me.

At some point, I wanted to tell people that Jason was my boyfriend – but I couldn't. It was an unusual form of torture, but it was one that I endured because I still had him. Even if the world didn't know it – Jason was still mine and I would have endured anything to keep it that way.

Before we really had a chance to address that problem though, we had to face another – Jason bloomed. Actually, that wasn't the problem so much as the side effects of it were. It seemed like everyone started to see him for the person I had always known him to be, and he enthralled everyone he met. His presence was so intoxicating and contagious that everyone wanted to be in his atmosphere – on his radar – by his side. Everyone wanted to be Jason's friend, but at the end of the day, he always made it clear I was the one who mattered to him.

Me.

He'd tried to bring me along with him into his world of popularity – but he became a man of the people, created by the people, and I wasn't what the people wanted. So, for two years I didn't say anything as Jason became more popular – joined the football team – went to parties – flirted with other girls. I knew that it didn't mean anything to him, and even though I thought about him nearly every second of the day, I still had my own life to live. I still had Michelle, the poetry club, volunteering, and my own hobbies – and even though those things didn't come close to filling the void Jason created, it was enough. So, I gave him space because there was nothing else I could do – but we'd been tied at the hip since the second grade and space was… a lot more miserable than I thought it would be.

Space bred doubt and jealousy and loneliness and fear – and all of that translated to anger because I was fifteen and I didn't know how to deal with the feeling of being replaced. So, I started arguments with Jason – pointless ones – the type where nobody wins but everyone feels justified in their opinions, so no apology is ever given, and no one kisses and makes up. He would retaliate by ignoring me in class and I would retaliate by ignoring him when he would text or call and snapping at him whenever we finally did talk. I did all this – not because I wanted to – but because I was hurting, and I wanted him to feel that way too, because he was breaking my heart, and I didn't know how to tell him that.

So, we went to war with each other instead.

But war is not a constant fight – it is a summation of battles that are either won or lost with pockets of peace hidden within it that make you wonder why you bother fighting each other in the first place. And those pockets of peace with Jason were blissful. During those times, it was like nothing had changed – we were still close, and we talked all the time, and he was still the person that I loved with all of who I was. Jason would spend all his free time with me and make me laugh for hours. We would hang out with Michelle and Lucas and I would feel like the world couldn't be any brighter than they were in those moments – that there was nothing more life could offer me because I already had everything I could ask for.

I was sixteen years old the first time I let Jason love me.

It hadn't been planned.

We were on a holiday break from school and we were both old enough to stay home alone while our parents went to work. It was expected that we would see each other – that we would meet up with Michelle and Lucas to see a movie or grab something to eat. It was an established fact that, given the opportunity, we would always choose to be together. But the long-standing rule for both our houses had always been that we weren't allowed inside if there was no adult present – because in all honesty, our parents didn't trust us – and that was a wise decision on their part because we didn't trust ourselves either.

It had been ten years since Jason became a part of my life and we'd only broken the rule once – that very first time in the eighth grade. We didn't break it again because we were both terrified of what would happen if we were alone like that again. Regardless of what our intentions were, I was always quick to give in to a bad idea – I was told they made for the best stories – so when Jason invited me inside, I didn't say no.

The original intention when I went over to his house was to ride with him to pick up Lucas and Michelle – but Lucas was sick, and Michelle was in Georgia with her dad. So, we ended up sitting outside just talking instead – which was harmless – but, when we got hungry, instead of ordering a pizza, he offered to make us sandwiches.

Inside.

Of course, I took him up on his offer.

It only made sense that we took the sandwiches to his room because we wanted to watch a movie while we ate.

It was only natural that he would sit a little too close to me – that I let him lace his fingers through mine – that I didn't question why we never turned on the TV or moved to pick up our plates.

Of all the things I had ever been, ignorant was not one of them.

I knew what was happening. The moment he asked if it was okay to shut the door and I agreed, my heart began racing in my chest. It had been so long since the last time Jason had held me, and I ached for his touch – his arms around my back holding me against his chest – his gentle touch on my chin lifting my face up so that his lips could reach mine. I knew what was happening and I did not stop him.

I didn't want to.

Not when his soft kisses strayed from my lips or when his hands undid the buttons of my shirt and certainly not when he caught his breath as my lips found the base of his throat. It didn't take long for his shirt to meet mine on the floor. He'd turned to back me into the door, and he was determined to have his mouth cover every inch of my skin that he could reach. My mind was in a foggy haze of pleasure where time passed like honey through an hourglass – slow but still faster than I wanted it to.

Even through the fog though, I could hear the buzzing. The systematic rhythm of a phone call – it was barely audible but rang like an alarm in my head. It made me aware of just how quiet it was in the room – aside from the sound of our heavy breathing and the rustle of clothes, there was nothing to break the silence. I met Jason's eyes and for a moment, time stopped.

His gaze bore into mine and I felt like he could see how hard my heart was pounding in my chest. He wasn't looking at me with a goofy grin or a charming smile like he normally did – no, he was looking at me like a man at the edge of his limit. I didn't know that look on his face or how to react to it – I just knew that I couldn't draw a steady breath under his gaze or stop the shockwaves going up and down my spine.

"Do you want to get that?"

It was a simple question, but I knew what he

was asking – and it had nothing to do with the phone call. He knew that if I wanted to answer it, I would. But I didn't.

He was asking permission.

Only the jeans we wore separated his warm flesh from mine and I could tell that wasn't a comfortable situation for him to be in – but he hadn't made a move to remedy it. In fact, he'd been careful to only put his hands in places they'd been before. Jason and I had pushed our limits on several occasions, but now we were tiptoeing a line that we'd never crossed before and would never be able to come back from.

If we stopped right now, there would still be time to retreat from it.

He wanted to know if I wanted to turn back because that is who Jason was – he was considerate. He was always more than happy to push my limits, but only if I wanted to – only if I let him. He wasn't going to push me into a situation that I wasn't comfortable with – no matter how much he may want to. He always showed restraint with me. But this wasn't a time where I needed that consideration, so I shook my head at him.

"I'll call them back later."

"Sure?"

I nodded and reached out to kiss him. That was all the confirmation he needed.

After that, the world around us faded away. My instincts took over and I followed his lead as we ventured into uncharted territory together. We learned each other in ways we'd never thought we would as we laid on his bedroom floor.

And with every passing kiss – passing touch – passing second, I fell more in love with Jason. Wrapped in his arms in a way no one else had ever been, I knew that whatever pain I endured on his behalf was worth it – even if all I got for my suffering was that moment – because in it, Jason showed me that he loved me.

And I believed him.

CHAPTER 7
& HIGH SCHOOL WAS NOT KIND TO US.

Loving Jason never got any easier.

We loved each other in every way we knew how. We thought we knew everything, but we were barely more than children and we didn't actually know anything at all – but you couldn't have told us that. It didn't matter that things became more complicated every time we were together – because we were seniors in high school and thriving off the promise that the world would be our oyster – it would fall at our feet – be for our taking. In ninety days, we would cross the stage into the real world and all that mattered to us was that we did it together.

We were naive in thinking that the worst was over – that our relationship had already made it through so much – that nothing else high school could throw at us would tear us apart. The problem was – our love was little more than a sandcastle on life's shore. We'd been careful to build up walls against the waves – but there was nothing we could do to protect against someone who wanted to kick down our castle.

That someone was named Alice Mayben.

I hated her with as much depth as I loved Jason. I wished her nothing good in this lifetime, or the next, or the one after that, because I was seventeen and loving Jason was painful enough without her – yet she had the audacity to try and lay claim to the person I decided belonged to me.

For six weeks, she and I fought over Jason – her trying to weasel her way into his heart and me trying to keep her out of it.

Jason entertained her and at that point, I should have let him go – but I was stubborn and refused to give her the satisfaction of thinking that she had replaced me. I knew Jason Orion Lipsky like she never would. I knew the boy from third grade who loved video games and chasing girls with spiders – the boy in sixth grade with braces who liked to hold my hand, and was afraid of dogs, but would jump in front of one to save me – the boy who cried on my shoulder in the eighth grade because his mom worked through Christmas and he couldn't bring his dad back from the dead – the boy who, even now, couldn't sleep unless he heard me wish him a good night.

Alice Mayben could not replace me.

It wasn't for her lack of trying though – she just didn't have the time. As the saying goes, Rome was not built in a day – neither was the type of relationship Jason and I had. He loved me more than anyone else – I never doubted that.

But I was done being loved only in secret.

After we reconciled for the last time, I somehow found myself in his bed. I always found myself in his bed – in his jeep – in his arms – and for a moment, I hated that his mother was a flight attendant. She was always gone and providing him with these opportune moments to prey on my weakness, because being alone with Jason was a bad idea I could never turn away from.

I was tired of Jason being my favorite bad idea – so I told him that I was done.

I was done with the games – the secrecy – the fighting and the arguing and the endless cycle of madness that always ended with us back in his bed with nothing changed. I told him that if he wanted to be with me, then he was going to have to choose me, and that would mean there would be no room for anyone else.

There was no room for Alice Mayben in the scheme of us being happy together.

It had been childish of me to fight with her in the first place. What did I look like getting jealous over a boy who played with girls? I wanted a man – and if Jason could not be that, then we would not be together. But I would not continue to disgrace myself by staying with a boy who expected me to fight over him – who didn't turn down the advances of other girls – who wasn't willing to let everyone know that I was his. My love was not a thing to be taken lightly. It was not given to be hidden away and ridiculed – to be played with – to only be returned to me in exchange for favors and discarded when it was inconvenient.

If Jason wanted to be with me, it was time he owned up to it – and not just where I could see.

Upon hearing that ultimatum, he didn't hesitate to choose me.

He told me that given his options, there was no choice to make. He told me that I was his world – that he couldn't imagine a life without me. Of his own accord, he asked to take me to prom to make up for everything – a proper date – not as his best friend but as the love of his life. I shouldn't have agreed to that – but I was a sucker for bad ideas, and this was by far the worst one.

I should have trusted my instincts. I should have turned Jason down. I should have left his bed, pulled on my clothes and walked away. But I was seventeen in the arms of the one I loved and I had yet to learn that men don't change that easily – that I had given him too many chances where an apology and a well-placed kiss were enough to earn my forgiveness – that I shouldn't believe any word that comes from a man's lips when I'm naked and vulnerable in his bed.

But I did.

I wanted to love Jason – I wanted him to love me as much as I loved him – so I gave him every ounce of my love that I possessed and presented it to him on a silver platter wrapped in a bow because, despite his track record telling me to do otherwise, I trusted him. I trusted his words when he promised me – I trusted his actions when he sealed it with a kiss – I trusted our history of unbroken promises.

Jason had never broken a sealed promise to me.

So, when the night finally arrived, I spent hours

getting ready. I'd spent the better part of the morning in the beauty shop – my soft, kinky curls getting straightened with a hot comb until they were a silky wave down my back. Michelle did my makeup for me at her house after we got our nails done – we talked nonstop about how the night would be the best one of our lives because she was going to be with Lucas, and I was going to be with Jason, and we'd make memories that would last a lifetime. We were all smiles and excited giggles when I left her house to go home and put on my dress. It was purple with a sweetheart neckline and stopped just above my knees. It had corset strings in the back that my mother helped to pull snug, and I wore it with the black wedge sandals that my father bought for me.

I was gorgeous.

It was the best I'd ever looked in my entire life, because I was going to be with Jason in front of everyone we knew at school – and if only for one night – I was going to be on his arm as his date, and not simply by his side as his best friend.

I imagined that night was going to be perfect. He would pick me up in the Benz he would borrow from his mom, and we would get Michelle and Lucas.

Then, we would go out to eat – somewhere more upscale than we normally went – maybe a Japanese steakhouse or something Italian – before heading to the hotel where prom was being held. He'd offer me his arm and like Cinderella, we would turn heads as we walked into the room – every eye would be on us – and the DJ – sensing the atmosphere – would play a slow song just for us and like prince charming himself, Jason would sweep me into his arms and lead me across the dance floor. We wouldn't be dancing anymore – we would be floating. His eyes would never leave mine as we swayed against each other, and as the music began to change to something faster and people crowded the floor – we would be the only ones standing still in the midst of so many moving bodies. He would kiss me and that would be the beginning of our happily ever after.

But that night never came because Jason never showed up.

I waited for over an hour and he never came. At first, I thought he was just late – but that didn't make sense because Jason was never late – and if he was, he always let me know. I checked my phone a thousand times – reset it – then checked it a thousand more.

No call.

No text.

Jason had forgotten about me.

Instead of going to my room though and having a good cry – like I should have – I got in my car and I drove myself to prom. No one saw me walk in – no heads turned my way – but I saw everything that I needed to.

Jason hadn't forgotten about me – he'd stood me up. He was not only there already – he was having the time of his life. I mean, why wouldn't he? It was only the last school dance of our lives. And if that wasn't enough – because there was no way that could be enough pain for one night – he was there with Alice Mayben. She was wearing a purple dress too – a floor length one that had to have been custom made for her because – even though I hated to admit it – she looked beautiful. I stood watching from the doorway with a poker face as they left the dance floor – as she sat in his lap – as she pressed her lips to his and smirked when she saw me.

Jason followed her gaze and we made eye contact for the only time we would that night – mine were bright with unshed tears, but his were those of a deer in headlights. I couldn't bear looking at his face, so I left.

I did not walk fast.

I gave Jason more than enough time to catch up to me – and a part of me wanted him to – because if he did and he apologized, I would forgive him for this transgression – because that is what I always did. But he didn't come after me. I drove home alone and went straight to my room. I took my dress off and stood in the shower until the water ran cold. I fell across my bed.

I cried.

I cried for every single thing that Jason had ever done to hurt me. I cried for the time he pushed me off the swings in the third grade – the time he lied about breaking my favorite pen in the fourth grade – the time he picked Miranda to be his partner for the three-legged race in the fifth grade – the time he gave Samantha the stuffed animal he won at the arcade because he knew I wanted it – all the summers he never texted me back or returned my phone calls until he felt like it – all the times he'd said he didn't have a girlfriend moments after stealing a kiss or confessing his love for me – all the times he went to parties without me then lied about even going – all the girls he'd kissed that weren't me – all the lies I stomached just because he told me he loved me and I believed him.

I cried for all the times I hurt him back – even though I was only hurting myself. I cried for the times I refused to play with him at recess in the fourth grade – for the times I ignored the seat he saved for me on the bus in the fifth grade – for the times I lied about being too busy when I knew he wanted to see me – for turning down his invitation to the eighth grade dance – for letting Jared walk me to class because I knew Jason hated him – for kissing Caleb in the hallway to get back at him for kissing Alice – for ignoring his phone calls and texts and feeling good that he was the one missing me for a change – for the times I lied about not having a boyfriend – for the times I lied about not loving him anymore – for the times I made him feel bad because I knew he loved me and I could.

I cried because I was seventeen and I had trusted Jason – had given him my heart – and I couldn't understand how we had gone from being best friends who did everything together to the twisted version of being in love that we were. I couldn't remember when, or even why, we started lying to each other – ignoring each other – using other people to hurt each other – all I knew was that I couldn't do it anymore. I had been a willing participant in this demented cycle for years. I hadn't been afraid to put my heart up as collateral because I thought every story had a happy ending – but every book I ever read, lied to me.

There was no happy ending to our story.

I do not end up with Jason. There was no amount of love in the world that could change that. The problem wasn't that I didn't love him or that he didn't love me – it just wasn't enough. Loving him wasn't enough to make me content to be his favorite girlfriend of many – or enough to keep Jason faithful to me – or enough to erase all the pain we caused each other – and it wasn't enough to make me stay.

Jason didn't love me enough to make me the only woman in his life, and I didn't love him enough to be okay with that.

So, that meant I had to let Jason go – uproot him from my heart – remove him from my mind – evict him from my life. For ten years I had put Jason first and thought about him in everything that I did, and it wasn't amounting to anything – my investments were coming up empty – I had nothing more to give that he hadn't already taken and broken and discarded. I would have done anything for Jason – anything at all – but not if he wasn't going to appreciate me – respect me – or love me the way that I deserved to be loved.

For three days straight, I did nothing but cry. I didn't eat – I didn't talk – I didn't leave my room at all. I didn't know how to function with the amount of pain – physical pain – I felt in my chest. I didn't want to know how to exist with it – I just wanted it to be gone.

Anger was the only immediate salve that could soothe the pain of heartbreak and I embraced it. Jason had done nothing to deserve me – he had caused me nothing but trouble since the day I met him – and though I had countless memories of his grin – I also knew my own face covered in tears far too well. There was a compassion inside of me that died – forgiveness was not something I was familiar with anymore – and I damn sure didn't have any patience left to entertain a boy and his childish games.

I submerged myself in a bubble of my own pain and fury, but as time tends to do – it passes. I skipped school on Monday – and despite how understanding my parents tried to be – they weren't going to let me risk graduation simply because I didn't show up for the last four weeks. They didn't know all of what was going on, but they weren't idiots – they knew I didn't go to prom with Jason as planned, and now I wouldn't see him or take his calls. That provided them with enough puzzle pieces to put things together.

School took priority over my broken heart though and on Tuesday, I was forced to go.

I did everything in my power to avoid Jason at school, which wasn't too hard because we only had one class together at the end of the day. I couldn't avoid him after the last bell though. My mother dropped me off that morning because she didn't trust me to drive myself to school – a wise move on her part – but I couldn't leave until she came to pick me up. That gave Jason plenty of time to find me and hang his arm over my shoulders like everything was fine.

"I've missed you."

I spun out from under his arm so fast that I bumped into a few people trying to get away from him. He followed me and a short chase ensued, but he caught up to me as I reached the stairs leading to the senior parking lot. My mom was planning to meet me there, but her car was nowhere in sight yet.

Jason caught my hand and held on to it when I tried to snatch it back from him.

"Hold on a second."

"Don't touch me!"

"Talk to me. Please."

Jason released my hand, but he maneuvered himself to block my exit. The stairs to the parking lot were narrow and Jason was a football player – even with my best efforts there was no way I was making it past him by force. A quick glance around let me know that we were alone and – though this would have been a desirable situation before – in that moment, I would have preferred kissing Alice Mayben myself. I took a step back – squared my shoulders – and prepared myself for this final conversation with him before I met his gaze. He looked concerned – confused even – and that infuriated me.

"You want to talk. So, talk."

"Why you so mad at me?"

"So, we're playing dumb?" I scoffed. "That's what we doing now?"

"Is it the Alice thing again?"

His tone of voice said everything to me. He was not concerned for me and my emotional well-being in the least. He thought this was something he would get away with – something he knew I would soon get over and he just wanted to get his apology out of the way. He wanted to skip to the part where he would coerce me back to his house – into his arms – into his bed – so that he could convince me that I was the only one he truly loved and I would forgive him for his actions proving otherwise. The fact that he was the one who chose to point out that Alice was not a new problem for us only served to stoke my anger.

How dare he assume I was a one-trick pony that only knew how to forgive him?

I shook my head as I looked at him. After a decade, I was embarrassed to think that my actions led him to believe that the woman he imagined me to be was the woman I truly was. A woman with no backbone – someone he could manipulate – a woman whose wrath was nothing for him to fear. He thought I would be loyal to him despite how he treated me – and I was smacked with the truth that he had every reason to believe that.

I was the one who stayed with him despite his attention diverting to Miranda, Samantha, Aaliyah, Ashley, Whitney, Jasmine, Mariah, and Alice. I was the one who gave him chance after chance to change his ways when we both knew that he never would. I was the one who held out hope that one day, he would treat me as his one and only, even after my gut told me that I was his default and not his first choice. I was the one who had so willingly played the part of the fool – so I had no right to be upset.

A fool is the type of girl I'd proven myself to be.

But a fool remains a fool only if you let them, and I was done being in love with a man who always made me out to be one.

"Listen, because I am not going to say this again," I said, taking a deep breath to calm myself enough to speak. "I am not your girlfriend. I am not your friend. I do not want you in my life anymore. I will never forgive you for the 'Alice thing'. I am done with this. Us. You. Everything. Pretend you don't know me."

"Kay –"

He didn't get to finish his next words because I slapped him across the face with all the force I had in my body. The sound echoed and the palm of my hand stung – I couldn't think through the sound of the blood rushing in my head – my heart was beating with enough force to make my vision jump with every beat.

Jason hadn't expected that – neither had I.

"Don't ever put my name in your mouth again."

I turned to take the long way around and use the stairs on the opposite side of the parking lot – Jason didn't stop me. My mom pulled into the parking lot as I finally made my way down, and I was pulling on the handle of the door before she came to a full stop. She glanced over at me before turning to look at Jason – he was watching us from the top of the stairs with a look on his face that resembled a dog being abandoned by its owner. She raised an eyebrow at me.

"You two okay?"

"No," I said as I buckled my seat belt. "We're not friends anymore."

"What happened?"

"Don't wanna talk about it," I mumbled.

She nodded her head as we pulled off and the conversation died there. I didn't mind though because I didn't want to talk to her about Jason. There was so much that she didn't know, and even more that I wouldn't have been able to tell her anyway. In fact, I never wanted to speak about Jason again – because even through the anger – I could still feel my heart rupturing with every mile put between us. He was the person I loved most in the world – who knew everything about me – who I'd imagined spending the rest of my life with – who was my best friend – and I'd just released my claim on him.

That gutted me like nothing else. Still though, I did not speak another word to Jason Orion Lipsky for five years.

CHAPTER 8
OUR STORY ISN'T THAT IM-PRESSIVE, BUT

"Damn. I can see why you don't tell people all that."

"Yep."

We looked at each other and I was filled with an uncontrollable laughter. Lana was confused by my reaction, but I couldn't help it. Her simple words in response to my deepest secret – my unending love for Jason – reminded me that I am not special in loving a man who excelled at breaking my heart. I wasn't unique – Jason wasn't different – I wasn't the only person in the world who ever felt like they deserved better than what they got. This was just another love story with a bad ending to her. It wasn't the first she's ever heard, and it probably wouldn't be the last – and though she may sympathize with my pain because she is my friend – it remains a collection of memories that have no impact on how she lives her life.

Jason didn't rock her world the way he did mine.

That wasn't surprising though – after all, he was just a man. I was the one who set myself up for failure when I set him up on a pedestal that he would never be able to stand on. Knowing that didn't make being without him hurt any less – didn't change the fact that I had spent my teenage years obsessing over him – didn't change the fact that my feelings for him still ran deeper than I was willing to swim.

Lana and I didn't speak anymore that night.

I woke up the next morning to the smell of coffee brewing. I pulled my body up from the couch and walked over to the small table in Lana's kitchen. The legs were uneven, so it wobbled a bit, but it was sturdy enough – she'd gotten it for free from the people across the hall who didn't want it anymore. For whatever reason, the table was green – it matched nothing she owned – and she swore that one day she would sand it down and repaint it, but that day had yet to come.

She placed a water bottle in front of me along with a cup of coffee and I stirred my own cream and sugar into it. I downed the water first – knowing that I needed to rehydrate after the previous night –

before lightly sipping the coffee. Lana set down some microwaved turkey bacon and toast in the center of the table before fixing her own cup of coffee and sitting across from me. Lana was the type of friend who was a natural mom – she took care of everyone else without a second thought and was the one I'd call if I needed advice, or help, or a hug.

Her curly black hair was pulled up into a pineapple bun with a satin scarf still wrapped around it – the entire thing shifted as she used a manicured finger to scratch her scalp and for whatever reason I found it amusing. She rolled her eyes at me before taking some of the turkey bacon and toast from the center.

"So," she said, ripping everything into bite sized pieces, "regarding your confession – what are you going to do?"

"I don't know. I honestly haven't given much thought to it."

"Liar."

I raised an eyebrow and paused in my reach for food. "What?"

"The way you talked about that man? There's no way you've never thought about what you would do if he just showed up one day."

I averted my eyes from her and focused on eating. Of course, she was right – but I didn't want to admit that. I spent most of my time combating my thoughts of Jason instead of thinking about how much I wanted to be with him again. The thought of seeing him again scrambled my brain so much that I ignored it altogether.

"I try not to think about him at all actually," I told her.

"That's your problem."

"What is?"

"You don't think about him," she said. "Honestly, he sounds like an asshole to me. I don't know what you see in him, but you talk like you still love him. And you just ran away from him." She shook her head. "It's no wonder you don't know what to do now – you never dealt with things in the first place."

"That's not true."

"Kam," she said with a straight face, "we've been best friends for what? Five years? And this is the first I've ever heard of him." I didn't say anything, and she sat back in her chair. "I mean, I don't fault you for not telling me about him. Like I said before, we all have our secrets – but if you're still feeling like this? I'm just saying," she shrugged, "you can't get over shit by pretending you don't feel the way you do."

"So, what?" I asked, "I'm just supposed to sit around and cry about it?"

"If you need to. Or talk to him. Or scream off a rooftop at the world. I don't know. I don't know what you need to do to deal with what you're feeling – but you need to feel it and deal with it. Repressing shit is not good for you."

"I'm not repressing –"

"You're repressing it," she interrupted me. "There's no reason you should be crying over a man you broke up with in high school like you just ended things yesterday. That's not normal. Deal with your problems Kam and stop ignoring them."

I simmered on her words for a moment before slowly nodding my head. "You're right. I'm not going to argue with you."

"Not like you could anyway."

"I'm trying to concede defeat here." She smirked but waved her hand for me to continue as she sipped her coffee. "As I said before," I emphasized, "you're right. I think I need to just talk to Jason and get some closure."

"Then do that."

"I will. We have plans to see each other in three weeks. I'll talk to him then."

CHAPTER 9
WE ALWAYS FIND OUR WAY BACK TOGETHER.

I'd be lying if I said that the next three weeks didn't feel like three months. Despite my normal distractions of work, Netflix, Lana and video games, I felt every minute of the time pass by. I was nervous to see Jason again – but I was also excited because I was going to see Jason again.

I still remembered the last time he invited me somewhere – just the two of us. We got two burgers and a bag of fries to split before we drove to the parking lot of an empty shopping center. We sat in the back watching the highway traffic as we ate. The radio played low, and we sat there talking and laughing until the sun went down.

Jason didn't love me in the backseat of his jeep that day.

Instead, he'd asked me to hold him. He put the seats in the back down, his head in my lap, and his arms around my waist. He just held onto me while I ran my fingers over his face trying to force my brain to burn every detail into my memory. I asked him if he was okay and he shook his head – said that his mother had a boyfriend – that her overnight trips kept getting longer and closer together – that home wasn't home anymore, it was just a house – that he was tired of being by himself. The only time he felt that he wasn't alone was when he was with me.

I kissed him on his forehead. I told him that I'd be with him as long as he wanted me – it was a lie I didn't know I was telling. I would only stay with him for a little more than two weeks – just until he took Alice Mayben to prom. After that, we would never have anything as pure as that moment again.

So, I didn't want to get my hopes up that Jason had changed. I had never been enough for him in the past and I wasn't sure if I was going to be enough for him now. But if I was being honest with myself – I wanted to be enough.

I wanted Jason.

I wanted all of him – not just the bits and pieces that were convenient to give – and I wanted all of him to myself. But I knew that if he couldn't be mine alone, then I would never be his again. I loved him – and though that wasn't reason enough to turn myself into another fool for him – I couldn't turn away from the possibility of turning our tragedy into a happily-ever-after.

Time works on everyone. I changed – maybe he did too.

So, when I walked into *The Diner on 3rd* and saw him sitting in a booth waiting for me, I knew that I'd walked onto the battlefield of a new war. With every step toward him that I took, my gut warned me that what was about to happen between us was not going to be easy – that this war would not be like the others – the battles would not be easily won. It would not be short-lived and there would be casualties – we would inflict wounds on each other that would ache for the rest of our lives and leave us with ugly scars – it would be impossible for us to leave as the same people we were entering into it, and still, my feet moved forward.

"Morning, Jason."

"Good morning," he said with a smile. He was sipping from a mug of coffee and looking over the menu when I slid into the seat across from him. I picked up the menu and glanced over it, but I already knew what I wanted to order.

The Diner on 3rd was a family-owned restaurant that only served breakfast and lunch. It had a classic look with black and white tile on the floor, ceramic mugs at every table, booths upholstered in red vinyl and a simple menu with the standard breakfast items. It wasn't a fancy place – it was a comfortable one that was never busy but also, never empty. Despite its name, it was off of Main Street, and it had windows on the front that showed the passing traffic. It had upbeat instrumentals playing through the speakers just loud enough to be heard and friendly waitresses who knew most people by name.

Elizabeth was the only one who didn't serve with a smile and I always sat in her section.

She was tall and thin with flawless brown skin, a shaved head, and she wore no makeup except for a clear gloss on lips that never smiled. She was twenty-one and only worked weekends at the diner – she never mentioned what she did during the week, but despite her cool demeanor, she was one of the most considerate people I'd ever run across.

I'd come in late one day as her last customer – a bad morning had rendered me unpleasant. She asked if I was alright and that, somehow, ended with her sitting across from me on her break, listening to me vent. She listened, nodded, told me everything would be fine, refilled my coffee and went back to work. Now, whenever I come in alone at the end of her shift, she sits and talks with me on her break.

She placed a fresh pot of coffee on the table with a bowl of cream. She pulled a notepad and pen from her pocket, glanced between us, before looking at Jason. Her eyebrow twitched upward as she looked at him.

"Welcome to the diner on third," she said. "Is this your first time here?"

"Yes."

She nodded. "Thanks for choosing to have breakfast with us. Are you ready to order?"

Jason's eyes darted to me. "Ladies first."

I looked toward Elizabeth and gave her a small smile. "Same thing as always for me."

"Two honey ham biscuits, two eggs over easy, side of grits." Elizabeth rattled off my order without much thought. She tapped her notebook with her pen as she turned her gaze back to Jason. He glanced at me and I shrugged.

"I'll have what she's having then," he said, handing the menu back to Elizabeth.

"Sure," she said, taking it and picking mine up from the table. "It'll be right out."

With Elizabeth and the menus gone there was nothing to distract Jason from me.

"You were late getting here," he said.

"I wasn't in much of a rush."

"You never have been."

I rolled my eyes. "Don't pretend you know me."

"I used to know you better than anyone."

"Yeah, well," I said, "don't forget I knew you too." I nodded toward the coffee cup he just refilled. "What number is that?"

"Two."

"And before you got here?"

"Let's just say my caffeine intake is sufficient."

He laughed and I couldn't stop the smile that spread on my face. His laugh was contagious, and I had no defense against it. I watched as he sipped his cup and remembered that Jason used to have the worst insomnia – he'd spend days running on nothing but five or six hours of sleep. To make up for his lack of sleep, he would drink so much caffeine that just watching him consume it all made me feel jittery. It was only on the days we spent together after school that he managed to get more than two hours of consecutive sleep.

It started in the eighth grade when his mom started leaving him alone to work overnight trips. She thought he was old enough to handle being alone until she came back, and she needed the hours – and he knew my parents were right down the street if something happened. He never adjusted to being alone though. After that, some days he would come over to my house after school just so he could sleep on the floor in my room knowing that someone would be there when he woke up.

Jason hated being alone more than anything else.

"When did you start eating eggs any other way than scrambled?"

His question pulled me from my thoughts, and I stirred my coffee as I thought about it. I had always been considered a somewhat picky eater – I was more than willing to try things, but once I did, I was quick to form an opinion about what I would and would not eat. Eggs had been unique in that, I ate them, but only scrambled.

"In college?"

"Is that a question or an answer?"

"I don't know," I said with a slight laugh. "I think it changed because I went out to eat with a friend once and got fried eggs when I ordered them scrambled. I was going to send them back, but they told me to just try them. I didn't hate them, so I kept trying them other ways." I smiled at him. "Nothing too crazy."

"Must be a pretty close friend if they got you to eat something new."

"Yeah," I nodded, "I guess they were."

Silence fell on us like a clumsy grade-schooler, and the air that was filled with easy conversation became thick with nerves and tension. We both sipped our coffee in silence. We hadn't been this awkward around each other since the sixth grade – back when our hormones started kicking in, and people kept questioning if we were going out when we didn't even know what that meant. I didn't know what to say. I avoided meeting Jason's eyes because I knew he was looking at me and the moment I did, I would lose my head – I always did.

"What's on your mind, Kay?"

I finally met his gaze when he said my name. It

felt nostalgic – but still, foreign to me at the same time. At one point it had been a familiar nickname – though, by junior year of high school, everyone had taken to calling me Kam instead. Jason was the only one who never changed, and I never got tired of hearing the sound of my name on his lips – no matter how he said it.

I didn't let many people call me that after Jason – it just didn't sound the same in someone else's voice. Hearing it now felt like getting stitches for a wound I didn't realize was still bleeding. I pulled on the end of one of my braids as I studied him.

"Why did you reach out to me?"

"What do you mean?"

"That email you sent," I clarified. "You didn't have to go out of your way to see me."

"Why wouldn't I?"

"Five years is a long time to not speak to someone."

He smirked. "You kept track of how long it was?"

"It's basic math," I said. I rolled my eyes, but my heart was pounding. Of course, I'd kept track.

"I guess it is," he said, sitting back in his seat. "I

emailed you because I wanted to. And when I found out that you were in the city I was moving to, I finally felt like I had an excuse. You were gone, but," he hesitated before saying his next words, like he was rethinking his sentence. He sighed before leaning forward again, locking his brown eyes onto mine. "I thought about you almost every day. I missed you, Kamry."

This was not a simple statement – it was a confession.

I didn't know what to do with a confession from Jason.

I was under the impression that he didn't miss me because all of his efforts to reach me ended within a week of our confrontation on the stairs – and not once had those efforts included a sincere apology. So, I was skeptical in believing his words now – because if I knew anything, I knew that Jason was a liar. I'd learned the hard way that he is adept at using his words to manipulate my feelings for him and I had no desire to be a butterfly caught in his spider's web.

Even knowing that, I wanted to believe him. I wanted to think that my absence from his life had shaken him to his core. I liked to think that his insomnia became a prison and he would find me in his dreams only to have reality become a nightmare he couldn't escape – that he would see me in the corner of his eye and that I would be gone when he turned to look my way – that his world would appear to him only in a grayscale until he imagined me in a purple dress he never got to see me wear only to learn that – I don't wear purple anymore. I wanted to believe that I'd been on his mind as much as he'd been on mine, and that absence makes the heart grow fonder, and that my heart wasn't racing for an impossible hope.

I wanted to believe Jason was ready for me this time.

Before I could think of a response, Elizabeth was walking over with our food and I couldn't help but think that her timing was perfect. It gave me a little more time to simmer on Jason's words and think of what I wanted to say – because I had no idea what words I could say to him without giving away how I really felt. I had missed him too, but that wasn't something I was willing to share with him yet.

"Y'all need anything else?"

We both looked at Elizabeth and shook our heads. She nodded, told us to let her know if we did need anything, and left. We started to eat our food in silence and before I could figure out what to say, Jason was speaking again.

"I don't expect you to have missed me too."

I paused. Jason was letting me off the hook. This wasn't something I expected from him. I picked up my fork and raised an eyebrow at him.

"You don't?"

He shook his head. "I was an asshole. I know that. Why would you miss me?"

"You do have a point there."

Our eyes met and we shared a smile as we began eating our food. It was quiet as we ate, but unlike before, it wasn't uncomfortable. It wasn't until we both were picking at what was left of our food that Jason looked up at me again.

"Sorry for being an asshole."

I nodded. "I accept your apology."

And just like that, the conversation started flowing again. I didn't have to overthink my words and I was reminded of just how effortless it had always been to talk to Jason – how effortless it still was. We sat there talking for hours. Elizabeth came by every so often to freshen up our coffee and refill our water glasses.

With every passing minute, it felt less and less like we were ever apart. That was the most terrifying aspect of everything though – how familiar it felt and how easy it was to fall back into the comfort of it all. Laughing with Jason on an early Saturday morning over coffee – it was like we'd gone back in time – or like time had never moved forward for us to begin with.

Jason said something that made me laugh again, and I was aware of how little I did that anymore. With him though, I was never quite able to catch my breath.

"I love the sound of your laugh."

"Careful there," I warned with a shake of my head. "It almost sounds like you still have feelings for me."

"And if I do?"

"This would not be the time or place to talk about it."

"What would be the time and place?"

His question was heavier than what I was prepared to lift – and for the second time that morning – I was left not knowing what to say. Jason smiled and pulled out his wallet.

"I don't need an answer right now," he said, placing two twenty-dollar bills on the table, "but think about it, okay?"

"Sure."

He smiled and offered to walk me to my car, but I declined. "I'm going to get an order to take home first."

"Okay," he said, as he stood from his seat. "Give me a call sometime, Kay. My number is still the same."

"I will."

The words were out of my mouth before I could think about what I was agreeing to. He grinned and held his arms out for a hug, and I wasn't strong enough to deny him, so I stood and let myself be folded into his embrace. I took a deep breath of his cologne and wrapped my arms around his waist. He held me for just a second too long – but I didn't move away either. When we pulled apart, he let his hand trail down my arm and across the tips of my fingers before saying he'd see me later and walking away. I watched him get into a black BMW before driving off.

Elizabeth walked over shortly after that and took down the order I wanted to-go. She brought back a small basket of rejected biscuits and set them down before sliding into the empty seat across from me.

"Was that your boyfriend?"

"Childhood friend," I corrected. "He just moved here from California," I said, abbreviating Jason's story.

"For you?"

"For work."

It was fun to imagine Jason moving across the country to be with me, but reality wasn't filled with such grand gestures. He was moving to put an end to the long distance, multi-time zone relationship he had with his business partner. Lucas and Michelle never split after they got together in college – and since she'd spent every summer, holiday, and school break that she could with her dad in Georgia – it came as no surprise that it's where she decided to move to after graduation. Lucas moved with her and they were renting a small house just outside the city.

I would have known that had I kept in touch with them, but I cut off everyone when I cut off Jason. I hadn't meant to include them in that, but they were the unfortunate casualties of war.

Elizabeth made a humming sound in the back of her throat as she helped herself to a biscuit and spread it with butter. "Y'all close?"

"Not anymore," I answered.

"Y'all seem close."

I shrugged. "Not anymore."

"Story there?"

I nodded. "A long one. It's not that interesting though."

"I wasn't big on listening to it."

She reached behind her to the next table over and grabbed an empty coffee cup before filling it from the pot she'd left on the table earlier. She left her coffee black, and she sipped on it as we both watched the traffic pass on Main Street. Or maybe she wasn't watching the street at all and was watching the parking lot instead – or the clouds – or something that only she could see. It was hard to tell with Elizabeth.

She was the type of woman who was non-intrusive and of few words – she didn't ask a lot of questions or push for information that wasn't offered – but she was good at just being present with people in the moments where they didn't want to be alone. She kept to herself the majority of the time and lived by the motto – it's none of my damn business. She was a direct contrast to Lana's bubbly, open-book nature.

"So," she asked, "not your boyfriend?"

"I wouldn't say that," I said after a slight pause. He wasn't, but I didn't want to give a definitive yes or no on the matter just yet.

"I see."

I turned to look at her. "Were you interested?"

"He is attractive, but no."

"No?"

She shook her head. "No."

We didn't say anything else as she took her break and ate the biscuits that were either overcooked or otherwise not worthy of being put out to customers. When her break was over, she stood and took the money Jason left for the bill before coming back with a receipt and my order.

"Thanks," I said, rising from my seat.

"No problem," she said, waving me off. "Be careful out there."

Part 2 – Kamry

My world collapsed in on itself the day that Kamry walked away from me. I had forced her over an edge there was no coming back from, and I've never experienced regret the way that I did that day. With each step she took away from me, I could pinpoint every single thing that I ever did wrong – there wasn't much I did right when it came to loving her.

I should have just loved her, but I was scared of Kamry.

She held my heart in her slender fingers and every smile of hers only tightened her grip on it. She was beautiful and fun and fearless, and she never shied away from a challenge. She had sunshine in her laughter – titanium in her spirit – clouds in her voice – and maybe that is what drew me to her. In a world of madness, she was peace – in the face of chaos, she was calm – in the middle of all life's storms, she was a sunny day. Third grade is when I knew I didn't want to live without her – sixth grade is when I realized I couldn't. I don't know how it happened, but it was so easy to become addicted to her. She wasn't a drug – but like walking – or laughing – being with her was such a natural part of being alive that I couldn't imagine what life would be like had I never met her.

Knowing that she had that kind of power over me, rattled my soul.

She was patient where most women would have given up on me – kind where most would have taken the opportunity to be cruel – unaffected by things that would anger anyone else. I knew she was reckless in loving me and that is what made loving her so difficult. She was the most precious thing in my life – but as a child, I treated her like a toy simply because I could. I played with her a little too much – set her aside to play with other toys, only to return to her when the newness wore off, because nothing could replace her. I saw the cracks I left on her as battle scars that marked her as mine, because I knew they couldn't be fixed. I treated her as indestructible only to cry over her with regret after she was broken.

I was too young to love Kamry.

A boy stood in the place where she deserved a man and I was merely pretending to be one – imagining that I was big enough to fill the shoes needed to walk beside her when – in reality, I couldn't even keep up with her. At the time, I was nothing more than a child – playing childish games – but as a man now, it is time to put away childish things.

I love Kamry Nicole Marshall with every fiber of my being.

I am no longer ashamed to admit that I need her in my life. I was a scarecrow missing a brain the first time around, but I will become a lion and find my courage because without her, I am a tinman without a heart – so I will pull back the curtain of my soul and show her who I am without all the smoke and mirrors and pray that she will still accept me.

And love me.

And stay with me.

Because, the best parts of myself cannot exist without her.

Chapter 10
Feelings This Strong Don't Fade,

Kamry.

No matter what I did, my mind kept drifting back to her. It would be an understatement to say I felt overwhelmed by the reality I was living. Moving to Georgia to keep working with Lucas hadn't been much of a decision – it was more of a necessity than anything else, and there wasn't much left for me in California anyway – but being around him and Michelle made my heart hurt for Kamry in ways that I thought it couldn't anymore.

It wasn't just being in love with her that I missed – I missed my best friend. I missed being able to talk to her whenever I wanted to. I missed the way her voice put me at ease – how she made me laugh even when I didn't want to – how she was able to see whatever problems I had with a clarity I never possessed. No matter the situation, Kamry was always confident in the path she took.

I missed the security that came in knowing that no matter what life threw at me, I could turn to her and she would be ready to fight the world with me.

Lucas had that with Michelle, and I envied the lucky bastard. It wasn't hard to tell that he was on the verge of worshipping the literal ground that she walked on – but he'd waited for her a long time. No other girl has shown up on his radar since our freshman year of college, but his efforts paid off during senior year when he worked up the courage to be honest with her about how he really felt. According to Michelle's retelling of the story though, she sighed of relief that he could finally ask her out.

Lucas was a quiet and reserved person – the complete opposite of me in every social aspect – but he was solid and reliable in ways I wish I could be. I never had to question if Lucas would come through for me if I needed him – if he was able, he would – and if he wasn't able, he'd still find a way. That's just the kind of person he was.

He didn't hesitate when I'd asked him to help me move. He'd moved to Georgia months ago with Michelle, but he still helped me haul boxes in the unforgiving heat without complaint. Michelle had lent a hand too and unpacked the basic things – like my kitchen and living room. Despite their help though, it would still be awhile before everything would be out of a box.

I groaned at the thought of how much was still left to be done. Just thinking about it made me more exhausted than I already was. So, instead of trying to cook something for dinner, I picked up my phone, googled the nearest pizza delivery and placed an order for a large pizza. As soon as I ended the call, my phone buzzed twice, but I was too tired to give it any attention. I ignored it and opted to take a shower instead.

It wasn't until I got out of the shower and had a pizza box in my lap that I realized how much of an idiot I was. The message was from an unknown number – not Lucas.

It was from Kamry.

I nearly dropped the pizza slice in my hand as my brain wrapped itself around the mistake I'd made. I sighed in frustration and read her message about four times before replying. My reply was over an hour late, so I didn't expect to get a response tonight – she was probably in bed or getting ready for it. It was a quarter till eleven and Kamry had always been a night-owl. Back in high school I'd learned her routine so I would know exactly the right time to call – after her parents were asleep, but before she was in bed. I wasn't sure if she'd changed or not, but if her routine was still the same, she'd have eaten dinner, cleaned up her room a bit and would be taking a shower about now – after she got out she'd play a game of some sort for an hour or two before calling it a night.

My mind tripped over the thought of her in the shower. Despite my best efforts to not imagine how different the woman I wanted now was from the girl I knew – my tired mind didn't have the will power to skip a ride on that train of thought. I couldn't help but picture her naked under the stream of water – droplets gliding down the pulse in the base of her throat and over the soft curve of her breast to get lost in the heated valley between her luscious thighs only to find its way down her never-ending legs. Just thinking about what she would look like with every inch of her golden-brown skin exposed put some energy back into my tired body – there wasn't much I wouldn't sacrifice to be able to have my hands trade places with those water droplets.

I was so deep in my thoughts I almost didn't hear the slight buzzing of my phone beside me. I picked it up to see a reply from Kamry. I couldn't stop the grin that spread across my face.

My phone was buzzing with conversation until midnight.

Kamry:
Hey. Thanks for breakfast this morning. You still awake?

Jason:
Yeah. I had to grab some dinner so I'm still up. And you're welcome to have breakfast on me anytime. Just let me know.

Kamry:
I'll keep that in mind lol. What did you grab for dinner?

Jason:
Pizza. From this place
Gino's I think. It's pretty
good.

Kamry:
Yeah? You still put
pineapple on your
pizza?

Jason:
Of course lol. You still
hate it?

Kamry:
There's honestly no
other way to feel
about it.
Kamry:
Jason, what are we
doing here?

Jason:
What do you mean?

Kamry:
I mean, what are we
doing? Why are we
talking to each other?

Keeping Promises

Jason:

Why not?

Kamry:

You know why not.

Don't avoid the

question.

Jason:

I missed you.

Jason:

Is that so crazy?

Kamry:

After five years? Yeah.

It is.

Jason:

I never stopped missing

you. I changed but not

so much that I forgot

you.

Kamry:

I reserve judgement

on that.

Jason:

On what? That I missed

you? Or that I changed?

Kamry:
Both.

Jason:
If it means you have to
spend more time with
me then judge all you
want.

Kamry:
I'm not spending any
more time with you
until we talk about
some things.

Jason:
We can talk about
anything.

Kamry:
Sure we can. Are you
free on Friday?

Jason:
Yeah.

Kamry:
Then plan to come by
my place. I'll send you
the address.

Keeping Promises

Jason:

Okay. I'll see you then.

Kamry:

Yeah. Goodnight.

Jason:

Night.

My heart was racing as I walked onto the balcony of my new apartment. It faced an inner courtyard that had a lounge area and a pool that turned the water different colors. I stood leaning against the railing, watching the water turn from green, to blue, to purple and pink, then yellow and back again. It was relaxing to watch the water – but despite how exhausted my body felt – my brain was working too much overtime for me to get any rest.

I took a deep breath of the humid night air and tried to slow the thoughts in my brain, but they were completely out of my control. I couldn't stop thinking about how the girl I loved grew into the woman I didn't want to lose twice.

I had no idea how to convince her that I missed her like a blinded man wanting to see the sun again, or a paralyzed man wanting to walk – and I definitely didn't know how to show her I'd changed. All I knew was that this was going to be a second – and final – chance to claim her for myself and I didn't want to let the opportunity go to waste.

"God! Why was I so stupid?"

It was a question – shout into the void of night that I had no answer to. I just stood there and beat the crap out of myself for treating her like I did. I ran tired hands over my face as I thought about how things ended up the way they were.

Chapter 11
Even Though I Was An Idiot,

Things started to go south for us in the fifth grade. I liked to think that high school is when everything went left for us, but I wasn't dumb enough to think that Alice was why Kamry left me – she was just the tip of the iceberg. No, our problems started long before high school was even on our radar – before we had cell phones and were worried about going to parties – before things were any more complicated than who to sit with at lunch.

It started at Kimner Elementary School with Miranda Leaf.

Miranda was the opposite of everything Kamry was. She was pale with blond hair and blue eyes – she wasn't all that smart or nice or funny – and she wasn't athletic either. I didn't like her at all, but she was pretty – and she always had a smile for me. She'd spread rumors about me and Kamry in the third grade, but by the fifth it all seemed like water under the bridge.

So, when she asked to be my partner for the three-legged race in gym, I agreed. It hadn't been the best idea, but Kamry had been ignoring me for the past few days – she said that she just wanted to hang out with Michelle for a change. In hindsight, I could understand that – I knew that her words weren't malicious – but they were arrows straight through the heart for me then. I'd been angry at her for not wanting to hang out with me instead, so I agreed to Miranda's request.

The moment was made all the sweeter when I saw Kamry running over to me.

I saw her face fall as Miranda grabbed my hand and pulled me over to where the teacher was. I watched as she looked around for anyone who didn't have a partner yet – because Michelle had already paired up with Lindsey and Lucas had paired up with Lacey. I felt smug as her irritation grew when she was paired up with Taylor – and I almost laughed at how angry she got when she lost the race because Taylor was slower than molasses in the middle of winter. It gave me my first taste of a twisted satisfaction – seeing her glare at Miranda whenever she could and having her rush over to me at the end of the day so

Miranda wouldn't have time to line up with me.

Kamry was jealous and I loved every minute of it.

I loved how her attention was focused only on me and what I was doing. It filled my stomach with jitters, and it made me happy to think that she wanted me to herself – that she wasn't going to let anyone else come between us. I was too young at the time to know that making someone jealous wears them down – that there's a limit to how much jealousy one person can tolerate – that it's a double-edged sword that would cut me to pieces if I wasn't careful – all I knew was that it was a powerful weapon that I'd just discovered.

If I wanted Kamry's attention, then all I had to do was talk to other girls.

By the sixth grade, I realized why I wanted all of Kamry's attention – my mom had teased me enough about her that I wasn't so clueless as to what I was feeling. I was in love with her. I'd ignored the feeling at first, but I didn't feel the same way whenever Lucas hung out with his brothers or when Michelle went to Georgia for the summer. It was only with Kamry. I wanted to hold her hand and be the only one she smiled so big at, and the only one who made her laugh until she cried. I didn't want anyone else to have her.

She was mine.

I'd started thinking of her that way in my head. It was nice to think that she felt the same way – we didn't say anything to each other, but she didn't pull away when I held her hand or put my arm around her shoulders or played with her curls in class. Kamry had the darkest, curliest hair I'd ever seen – and when she didn't have them in braids – she pulled it back into a slick puff. I almost always sat behind her and I loved pulling at the strands just to watch them bounce right back into place. Kamry always told me to stop, but I never listened, and she gave up on telling me to – just told me to not break her hair or stick anything in it.

I've never met any girl prettier than Kamry.

Her brown skin was smooth and looked like the sun was trapped beneath it – her brown eyes were clear and she never looked away from me when I was talking to her – her hands were soft and she had long fingers that she always kept painted in orange polish since it was her favorite color. Her smile was always genuine – her laugh was enough to brighten a room – her hugs were soft and warm and comforting, and she was never in a rush to let me go. She had a sharp tongue that could cut anyone down to size – a glare that could put frost in a person's veins – and she could hold grudges like it was her only lifeline out of hell, because she never knew what it meant to give anything less than her best.

She wasn't perfect – but my God, was that girl amazing.

She was the type of person to keep to herself – but when you got to really know her, she opened up like a flower in full bloom – and everyone got taken in by a person like that. Jared Mitchell was the first person to make me realize that I wasn't the only one with his eye on her. In the seventh grade, I remember Jared talking about her in the locker room – said that he was going to try to talk to her.

I told him she wouldn't be interested.

He said she could tell him that herself.

I told him to forget it.

He told me to make him.

So, I shoved him into the lockers.

It wasn't the best move to make on my part. I was ticked off though – I didn't want him getting near Kamry – I didn't want any competition from him or anyone else. The coach came in and we separated – and I all but forgot that moment.

It wasn't until Kamry breezed past me one Monday morning almost a year later to meet him in the hallway that I remembered it. Lucas had invited all of us to go bowling with his family on Saturday and while we were there, I won enough tickets in the arcade there to get a giant stuffed bunny as the prize. Kamry made it no secret that she wanted it. I won it with the express purpose of giving it to her – but every time it was her turn to bowl, I saw her talking and laughing with Lucas' older brother, Logan.

It didn't bother me until Logan started going up to the line with her to show her how to bowl a strike and started sharing food with her. Looking back on it – it was immature of me to get angry. Logan had been in the tenth grade at the time and he wasn't treating Kamry any different than he was treating Michelle or Samantha – his little sister. That day though, I felt like he was flirting with Kamry and she was letting him. So, when she saw I'd won the bunny, her eyes lit up only for her face to fall when I handed it over to Samantha.

It was no secret that Samantha had a crush on me

– don't all little sisters crush on their older brother's friends at some point? So, she squealed with delight when I handed it to her, and she hugged me before going over to giggle about it with her friends. She was my shadow for the rest of the day, and that was the first time I'd been on the receiving end of Kamry's glare. It sent chills down my spine, but it also felt good to make her feel like I'd been feeling all day.

She didn't speak to me for the rest of the day or over the weekend, and on Monday she ignored me to smile up at Jared instead. He offered to walk with her to her next class – and she nodded at him – but she made eye contact with me before walking off, and I knew then that her actions had been intentional.

Jared was her retribution for Samantha.

I learned that week that jealousy was a double-edged sword and I'd been cut deep. All week, she ignored me to hang out with Jared – I tried to play it cool, but I couldn't stomach it when he started draping his arm around her shoulders. On Friday, I apologized to her – on Saturday things went back to normal – on Sunday, I asked her out and kissed her for the first time.

I was an idiot to think that would fix anything.

Chapter 12
& I never deserved her,

By the time high school rolled around, we were stuck in a wash – rinse – repeat cycle of hurting each other. She would talk to the wrong people – flirt with some other guy – make me feel insecure – like she'd lost interest in me, and I would reciprocate by flirting with someone else.

Aaliyah – she was too easy.

Ashley – she was full of drama.

Whitney – she was just evil.

And each time Kamry would react the way I wanted her to. She'd get jealous – get mad – get clingy to me. As we got older, I became more popular and finding other girls just became easier – I didn't need to work for it. I only had to look at one the right way – smile at her – hold the door or show a mild level of interest and they were hooked.

Maybe it started going to my head – maybe I just liked that it was so easy to do – or maybe I just liked having their attention and the guys I hung out with changed girlfriends as often as the calendar changed months – but I couldn't stop. Even when Kamry did nothing to provoke me, I found my eyes wandering to other girls.

Jasmine had a fat ass, but she was too short.

Mariah was extra curvy, but she wouldn't tolerate being second to Kamry.

Alice was a bitch.

She was the only girl in high school who could've rivaled Kamry for how pretty she was, in my eyes. Maybe it was her onyx skin or her short platinum hair or her hourglass frame that did it for me, but I knew that everything beautiful about her was only skin deep – when I was seventeen though, that was enough.

From the beginning, I'd known what she was trying to do. She'd made it clear that she wanted to be my number one – that she had no interest in playing second fiddle to Kamry Marshall – that she would do everything in her power to make me forget about her. Now, in some part of my brain, I knew that Alice was nothing but trouble – that messing with her would push Kamry way beyond jealousy – that she was crossing a line.

There had always been a clear distinction in my

mind between Kamry and other girls and Alice was blurring it.

She was aggressive where Kamry wasn't – outgoing where Kamry was reserved – bold where Kamry would've been shy. She was horrible in so many ways, but she was enticing – and popular – and the girl everyone said I should be with – and she was willing to do things in places that Kamry just wouldn't.

If Kamry was an angel, then Alice was a demon.

I liked to blame her for ruining things – it was easier on me that way – but she'd been nothing more than a girl playing games of her own, with a boy who'd already overplayed his hand with a woman who was fast losing interest in him.

I knew that Kamry was getting tired of the games. She'd said as much on several occasions, but she still entertained them with me, so I kept playing them. But she was outgrowing me – I could feel it. She kept looking toward the future and making plans for herself that no longer revolved around me – and I was terrified.

I felt like she would leave me behind and I couldn't fathom what a world without Kamry would be like. But college was looming on the horizon and time waits for no man.

I'd been awake for about two days straight when she gave me her ultimatum – her or Alice. I chose her because she is the one that I wanted. Despite my horrid actions – despite causing her pain and going out of my way to make her jealous – I loved Kamry. She was the only girl I loved and wanted to be with. That had been true since the sixth grade and even as we neared graduation it remained true.

It's why I always went running back to her.

And when I was as dead tired as I was, my brain couldn't move fast enough to lie. So, I told her my unfiltered truth. I loved her. I'd always loved her. I would love her until my dying breath and even beyond the grave. She was my entire world and Alice was nothing compared to her. I begged her to let me take her to prom. She agreed.

For the two weeks leading up to prom night, I was king of the world – nothing could bring me down. I had the love of my life in my dreams and in my bed and I would be taking her on the best date of her life, and we would finally get to the happy ending that we wanted.

Keeping Promises

That is, until things went sideways.

Under normal circumstances, I didn't hang out with Kyle from the football team. Mostly because he was a bad dude with bad vibes who made bad choices. But his girlfriend, Destiny, was best friends with Alice – that should've been a warning – and when I went to tell her I was done with her, we ended up smoking whatever Kyle had on him, and I got caught up with her instead. Until that day, we'd never gone any further than Alice being on her knees. Despite my terrible lapses in judgement, I felt there was a strict line between messing around on Kamry and straight up cheating on her, and I'd never straight up cheated on her – until then.

I tried to tell her that was our last hurrah – she said it wasn't.

She demanded that I take her to prom, or she'd show Kamry the pictures she'd taken – because of course the sneaky bitch had taken pictures. For two days I anguished over what to do. I could tell Kamry what happened and pray she'd forgive me – but I knew she wouldn't. I'd screwed up too many times before and she wouldn't believe me if I told her the truth – that none of it had been intentional and I'd just been high on some shit I shouldn't have smoked – that I went over there to tell Alice to leave us – to leave her – alone.

My only other option was to take Alice to prom and then apologize to Kamry later.

It was a coward's move to not tell Kamry, but when I was seventeen, it seemed like the best thing to do. I hadn't expected that Alice would kiss me in front of everyone. I couldn't have predicted that Kamry would show up at the worst possible time and see her do it.

I tried to go after her, but Alice grinned – waving her phone in front of my face, reminding me of the threat I had no doubt she would follow through on.

It took everything in me to not rock her jaw where we stood. I'd never hit a woman – would never hit a woman – but had Lucas not pulled me away in that moment, I might have. I was only human, and she was finding a sick delight in ruining the best thing in my life simply because she could.

Kamry didn't come to school on Monday. She avoided me all day on Tuesday and when I finally caught up with her, I tried to downplay what happened in an effort to keep things under control.

That only pissed her off more though, and she was already livid. She told me that she was done with me – that she didn't want me in her life – that I should pretend I didn't know her. My chest tightened at each of her words and I tried to keep her from leaving, but before I could even get her name out of my mouth, she slapped me across the face as hard as she could.

I sighed as my fingers rubbed over my left cheek. It had been over five years since that day on the stairs – and I still remembered the sting of her palm against my face – but it was nothing compared to the pain I felt as she walked away from me. My chest still tightened whenever I thought about the look she had in her eye that day – one of complete fury and rage – and though her words had been calm, they still echoed around in my head like they'd been shouted into an empty cave, and they reminded me the cost of my actions.

I broke the only girl who'd ever loved me.

Even as my world crumbled around me with every step she took, I didn't have it in me to be angry with her – how could I? She'd only been patient, understanding, and forgiving for ten years while she showered me with love, attention, and affection. She was never shy about letting me know her feelings – that I was important to her – that she loved me – and she did it out of sincerity. She never used her love for me as a weapon against me – and for that alone, I didn't deserve her – because I can't say that I wasn't guilty of the same thing.

"I should've just told her the truth."

It was the clarity that came with hindsight. I should've told Kamry the truth. I shouldn't have gone to see Alice that day – I damn sure shouldn't have accepted anything Kyle gave me – I shouldn't have even entertained Alice to begin with. Or Mariah – or Jasmine – or Samantha – or Miranda – or any of the girls I made her suffer through.

It cost me my best friend in the end, and none of it was worth that.

Because, despite being as successful as a self-employed man could hope to be at my age, not having anyone to share it with made everything feel somewhat empty. There were plenty of women who were willing to share their bed with me – that much hadn't changed – but there few who were willing to spend their time and I wanted more than just a quick roll in the sheets. And – if I was being honest to the fullest extent – I was over the idea of getting attention from any woman who wasn't Kamry Nicole Marshall. My weakness for other women is what drove Kamry away from me in the first place and I wasn't much interested in continuing the habit – especially since I was getting a second chance with her.

Kamry was the only woman I wanted – then and now – and there was no point settling for anyone who made me feel anything less than what I felt for her.

I'd put effort into trying to forget her – but I was done lying to myself about how I felt about her. She was the only woman who ever knew me better than I knew myself – who loved me without requirement – who had loved me long before I was successful and making money, before I was popular, before I was even cool. She wasn't the type of woman to be swayed or impressed by anything I had – she would see me only as a man and not as a tool or accessory to use for her own gain.

At some point, I dragged myself to bed with her still on my mind – I was determined to get some rest even if sleep never found me. It wasn't until my body was too heavy to lift anymore and the sun started to slip through the slats on the blinds that I faced the truth of my situation. Sending that email to her old email address had been a gamble that paid off – I was meeting Kamry at her house on Friday for what was going to be my last chance to fix things with her. There would no doubt be an epic removal of skeletons from our metaphorical closet – which meant there would be no secrets left for me to keep to myself.

She was going to know everything and there was no time left for me to be scared. I wanted her more than my next breath, so I would have to face her and accept the repercussions of all the damage I caused. I was ready for anything though because I had never – not even for a minute – stopped loving her.

Hey Kay,

It's Jason. Your mom told my mom who told me you live in Georgia now. I'm moving out there in a month for work, so I'll be there apartment shopping next week. I googled the city and there's this café called Coffee Cakes near the area I'm planning to move to. I would love to buy you a cup of coffee if you have the time. I'll take a single minute if that's all you've got.

I'll leave the address down below. I'll be there around nine on Saturday. I hope to see you there.

Sincerely,

Jason

Part 3 – Us

It was so surprising to me when my life continued after I broke up with Jason. I'd convinced myself that not having him in my life was the same as not having a life at all. Before I walked away from him – my breath quick and the center of my palm stinging – I would never have believed that seconds would still tick by on the clock. I believed that – similar to closing a book – there would be nothing after the end.

It's laughable to think I was willing to put that much power over myself – over my existence – into the hands of someone else – let alone, a man who didn't even deserve my time. How silly I'd been to imagine the hands of the clock would bend to my emotions – that the sun would slow its rising to match the pace of my broken heart – that life was fair and forgiving and willing to let me sign out of it while I got myself together. I was too young to realize how naive I was.

My life did not end with leaving Jason – that is the point where it began.

In the moment that I left him standing there at the top of the stairs – I began to grow into the person I would become. And like a child realizing that the Easter bunny is a myth – that the tooth fairy is a lie – that good ol' Saint Nick has been dead for centuries – my eyes were opened to a truth that I'd been too blinded by love to see all along.

I was not as unpopular as I always believed myself to be.

I'd thought my only appeal was being close to Jason – because everyone wanted to be close to Jason – and I would never be seen as more than his shadow as long as I remained by his side. But without him, I shined. And I realized that Jason was no more than a lampshade – his presence only served to hide me – to dim me – to surround me so that, when heads turned my way, they'd see him first. I was less his lover and more of a bird in the palm of his hand – his fingers were slow to curl into a cage around me – but his true purpose was only to keep me within his grasp. All the time we'd been together, I thought I was the one who wanted to keep him close – but he was the one afraid of losing me.

It's true that I was the girl who never made waves

– but that is because I was the eye of the storm. I was powerful and a force of nature in my own right and I could not – and would not – be stopped or held back by a man who was incapable of loving me properly. I amazed people when I was nothing more than myself – when I was no longer restricted by playing the role of Jason's friend – when I was no longer a bird who thought the world existed only within the confines of its cage.

I terrified those who were not ready for me.

In all honesty I don't even know if I was ready for myself. I was changing before my own eyes and I didn't know if I was becoming this new person – or if this new person is who I had been all along, and I'd just been pretending to be someone else. Either way, I learned things about myself that were new to me.

I was unforgiving – I'd given every bit of my patience and understanding to Jason so there was none left for anyone else. I was distant – I didn't want to give up parts of myself to others who were undeserving of me. I was selective in who I deemed worthy of my time – after spending years with Jason, I didn't have seconds to spare on anyone who would waste them. I was blunt, uncaring, dismissive of boys pretending to be men, and a liar – because when asked about Jason, I'd say that I didn't know him.

I was Kamry – and Jason was a being who no longer existed in my universe. If I wasn't enough for anyone on my own – that only meant my presence was too much for them – and I'd learned not to lower my standards to accommodate people who weren't ready for me.

I destroyed the weak men who crossed my path – because one man like Jason was enough for a lifetime.

CHAPTER 13
& THE SPARK BETWEEN US
COULD NEVER DIE.

When Friday night rolled around, I was nervous. I could feel the energy pumping through my veins, and I kept walking around my apartment – just going back and forth – moving things around only to return them back to their original places. I never imagined that the time would come when I'd be willing to hear Jason out and – depending on what he said – give him another chance.

My heart was beating faster than normal, and I was already frustrated with myself for having such a knee-jerk reaction to him. Jason was just a man – and I wasn't a novice when it came to dealing with men anymore – but somehow, he was evading all of my precautionary measures just by being present in my life. Regardless though, I was ready for whatever would happen. Jason had been on my mind, nonstop for the entire week – and I was ready for some type of resolution to things – whatever the outcome may be. For all the effort I put into running countless scenarios in my head – I knew there was no way to predict how things would turn out.

Jason was too much of an unpredictable variable.

He made it clear enough that he wanted to be back in my life – and I wasn't naive enough anymore to think that he just wanted to be friends. I'd be lying if I said I didn't think about it – think about being alone with him – think about how easily things could lead me to pushing him through either the front door or into my bed – think about how much I still wanted him.

But we hadn't ended things on good terms – especially from my perspective. I wasn't unwilling to give him a chance at this point, but there were a lot of things that needed to be resolved. We'd already spent too much time in each other's company for things to still be left unsaid.

I would not spend another second with Jason if he was trying to replicate the relationship we had before – there would be nothing to talk about.

I wasn't interested in hearing excuses or apologies – what's been done has been done and nothing would undo it. What I wanted was acknowledgement – that we'd hurt each other – that we'd screwed things up in the worst kind of way – that if I let him back into my life, things would be different this time around and I wouldn't walk away from all this with an irreparable heart. I wasn't the same girl he knew who was willing to accept whatever he was willing to give – and as a woman, I'd learned to never negotiate the terms of my expectations.

I demanded respect.

It was a key element we were both lacking in high school and it wasn't something I was willing to compromise on. I knew who I was without him. I wasn't going to entertain his games or lose myself in who he was ever again – and if his expectation was that I would follow along behind him like I did before – reality was going to have a field day beating the crap out of him.

A future with Jason was a dream I'd given up on – and I didn't want it so bad now that I would risk everything to be in a relationship with him like I did last time. I wasn't reckless with my heart anymore.

Three soft knocks came at my door a few minutes after seven, and I took a deep breath as I stood from the couch to let him in.

"Hi, Jason."

It would be an understatement to say that things were awkward when he first walked in. He sort of stood by the door as I shut it behind him and looked around. My apartment wasn't big, and I didn't have a bunch of furniture outside of the standard bar stools, couch, coffee table and tv-stand. There was a little hallway off to the side that led to my bedroom on the left and the bathroom on the right. It wasn't until I questioned him about the paper bag that smelled like food that he moved further inside.

"Burgers," he stated, placing the bag on the counter. "I didn't know if you'd had any food yet, so I picked these up on the way over."

I walked over to him as he began taking things out. He stole a fry from the bottom of the bag as he placed my food next to his, and I couldn't stop the smile that spread across my face as I unwrapped it.

"Extra pickles and mayo?"

He nodded. "Extra pickle and mayo – no salt on the fries – ketchup is in the bag."

I shook my head in surprise as I looked at him. "I can't believe you remembered that."

"How could I forget? It's the only type of burger you ordered. It didn't matter where we went," he laughed.

I picked up my share of the food and he followed me to the couch, and we ate at the coffee table. I enjoyed every bite of the greasy mess in front of me – it hit a craving I didn't even know I had. I'd stopped eating out so much as I got older – mostly because it was expensive, and I didn't work out as often as I probably should – but a good burger was something I missed from time to time and this tasted better than I remember them being.

It probably had something to do with the fact I was feeling some convoluted emotions because Jason had remembered my order all the way down to the unsalted fries. I grabbed us some water bottles from the fridge and we ate in silence. I was grateful for the distraction and the food – I didn't really know how to start the conversation that I wanted – but there came a time for everything and soon the food was gone. I threw away the wrappers and the bag and sunk into the opposite side of the couch.

For a moment we just sat staring at each other, wondering who was going to break the ice first.

"You said we needed to talk," he offered into the silence.

"I did."

"So…" he shrugged, "you want to talk?"

I laughed at how unnerving the situation felt and decided to just dive into it. There was honestly no other way to handle the situation and worrying about it wasn't going to help anyone.

"Yeah. So." I paused and sighed. "I don't really know how to ask this, so I'm just going to ask it. What are you expecting from spending time with me?"

"What do you mean?"

"Exactly what I said." I took a deep breath. "You said in the diner that you missed me. That you thought about me and that you still had feelings for me. You're apologizing and telling me that you've changed, and I don't know what to make of what you're telling me." I paused and studied his face. "You can imagine that I would have a hard time believing you, right?"

"I don't see why you would."

"Jason, be serious here."

"I am serious. I've never once lied about loving you, Kay," he said with a shrug. "I went about it the wrong way before, but it doesn't change how I felt about you. I was just young and stupid."

"And what are you now?"

"Probably still young and stupid," he grinned. "But not so stupid as to need the same lesson twice. You left once and that was enough."

"Enough for what exactly?"

"Enough for me to know that I want you in my life and I'm willing to do whatever it takes to make sure you stay in it." I stared at him not quite knowing what to say and he leaned forward, staring back at me. "Look, Kamry," he finally said, "I'm not here to play games with you, okay? So, if that's what you're worried about, don't be."

"Yeah," I said slowly stretching out the word as I tried to put my thoughts in order, "that sounds nice and everything, but," I shrugged, "we both know that you excel at getting me to believe things that aren't necessarily true."

"I fucked up," he said with a nod. "I don't blame you for not trusting me. But all I can do right now is tell you the truth. I never stopped loving you – I still love you – and I'll do whatever you want if it means I can get another chance."

I sat there, marinating on his words. I wanted to forgive him – but that has always been my biggest weakness – I was always willing to forgive Jason. Time, apparently, had not changed that for me. Nor did it change the fact that I wanted to believe his words – wanted to hear that he loved me – wanted to know that he regretted his actions that led to him not being with me. And even though he'd won this battle, I still wanted him to beg just a little bit longer.

"Another chance? Do you know how many of those I gave you that you wasted?"

"I know."

"Do you?" My voice shot up at least two octaves and I shook my head. "Because right now you're looking me in my face and asking for yet another one because, what? You finally realized that I'm amazing and you can't replace me?"

"I don't know what you want me to say."

"Me either," I said.

After a few moments of silence, he spoke up again.

"How do you feel?"

"I feel like it's not fair that it took you this long to realize that you fucked up." I sighed, "But better late than never I guess." I studied his face. "But let me be clear, Jason. This is a final chance. You fuck this up and that's it. There's no room for you to try and convince me of anything else."

"Okay," he said moving down the couch closer to me.

"And I'm not the same, Jason," I warned him, placing my hand on his shoulder. "So, don't expect things to be like they were before. If you think that I'm going to tolerate your bullshit for even a second, you can leave right now."

"If you think I'm leaving now, you're crazy."

"We still have a lot of things we need to work out."

"Yeah. Later."

"And we still –"

"Kamry," he interrupted. "I'm not going anywhere. We have time to work out all the details — as many as you want. So, please. Just stop talking and come here."

There was no space left for words as his lips covered mine – and like the first time he kissed me in the eighth-grade, shockwaves raced up and down my spine. This time though, I kissed him back – I held him closer, and I didn't get scared when his hands moved to push my shirt aside. This time, he didn't need to ask for permission and I didn't hesitate to let myself get lost in the feel of his body – and like puzzle pieces fitting back into their proper places, we made a picture of love that hadn't been complete in half a decade.

His tongue was hot on my skin.

His hands traveled paths that only his fingers knew – caressed the places that he'd been the first to discover – reminded my body of the touch that was nearly forgotten. I couldn't think – I could barely breathe – the only strength I had left in my body was used to cling to him. I'd forgotten how well he could use his silver tongue to take my breath away. And even though he was the same person who loved me first – loving him was different now. I wasn't afraid to make waves anymore, so he learned to surf – and he was still a rollercoaster ride I couldn't stop, so I just screamed when I reached the top – and if all of this ended in pain it would be well worth it, because Jason was finally mine to love.

He always made it impossible for me to let him go and time didn't change that. I wanted to love Jason because I loved loving Jason – so that is what I did until Monday morning made itself known. We had five years of missed time to make up for – and he was a bad idea that I no longer felt guilty about giving in to – so, I let myself enjoy every part of him until I had my fill.

I loved that man.

I was in love with him. He was in love with me. We'd loved each other our entire lives.

He was bold in promising to love me forever, and I warned him to mind his words if he wasn't certain his actions would follow, because I didn't need any more broken promises falling from his lips. His only response was to silence my rebuttal with a well-placed kiss and tell me again that he would love me until every star lost its light – until the earth fell off its axis – until infinity reached the end – until the alphabet no longer knew how to make words.

And like every other time before – I believed him.

I didn't have any defenses to use against Jason. I never had. Loving him came so naturally to me that it was both the easiest and hardest thing I've ever had to do. I didn't have to think about it, but I knew that

Keeping Promises

I wouldn't be able to stop – even if I wanted to. As Friday night turned into Saturday morning though, I realized I was okay with that because I had something the rest of the world didn't.

I had Jason.

Thank You

If you enjoyed **Keeping Promises**, please recommend it to a friend and consider leaving a review on Amazon.

Check out Written in Melanin on YouTube at
YouTube.com/c/WrittenInMelanin

Follow me on Twitter and Instagram
@CLockhartWrite
@WrittenNMelanin

To learn more, head over to
WrittenInMelanin.com

For more books by Black authors, visit
MelaninLibrary.com

Acknowledgments

To Benjamin – you are the biggest blessing in my life. You encouraged me and believed in me before I believed in myself. I will love you forever – beyond the boundaries of time and existence – so if we're wrong about everything, and reincarnation is real – I promise to do everything I can to find you in every lifetime that I get.

Now, let me tell you something – this book would not exist without you. For every word, draft, edit, option and idea straight out of left field that I ran by you – for being patient and not so patient with me at all times of the day or night – for calming my anxiety and being honest and always present in my life – I can't thank you enough.

I hope I die before you so that I never have to live without you.

To all the amazing people in the Melanin Network that I've met in the two years since the original release of this book – Audra, DL, LaKase, Tristan, Celeste, Porsha, everyone – y'all are absolutely amazing people and I'm so grateful to have found a community with you. Please know that I'm rooting for you as loudly as I possibly can.

About the Author

C. M. Lockhart is a woman with a passion for tea, laughter, and words. She believes that the greatest feeling in the world is to be able to find yourself reflected within the pages of a book – so that is what she aspires to give to her readers. Aside from writing, she enjoys watching anime, playing video games, and listening to music. She is the founder of the Melanin Library and currently lives in North Carolina with her husband and dog.

She was once told that she is the tornado in the Wizard of Oz and she can't think of a compliment better than that.